GORGER

Paul G. Andrews

dizzyemupublishing.com

DIZZY EMU PUBLISHING

1714 N McCadden Place, Hollywood, Los Angeles 90028

dizzyemupublishing.com

Gorger
Paul G. Andrews

First published in the United States
in 2022 by Dizzy Emu Publishing

Copyright © Paul G. Andrews 2022

Paul G. Andrews has asserted his right under the
Copyright, Designs and Patents Act 1988 to be
identified as the author of this work.

1 3 5 7 9 10 8 6 4 2

This book is sold subject to the condition that it
shall not, by way of trade or otherwise, be lent,
resold, hired out, or otherwise circulated without the
publisher's prior consent in any form of binding or
cover other than that in which it is published and
without a similar condition, including this condition,
being imposed on the subsequent purchaser.

dizzyemupublishing.com

GORGER

Paul G. Andrews

GORGER

Written by

Paul G. Andrews

based upon an original idea by
David Appleton

Copyright 2022 GlobalWatch
Producer : Paul G Andrews
pandrews@globalwatch.com
WGA Registered

EXT. METAL EXCHANGE AND DEPOSIT, LONDON - NIGHT

An imposing brick building. In the back, a small van idles, the name "EAST END HYGIENE" painted on the side.

In the driver's seat sits the nervous QUINLAN HEARN, 27, scanning the alley back and forth. He has the exotic good looks of his British Gypsy/Traveller heritage.

INT. VAULT, METAL EXCHANGE AND DEPOSIT - NIGHT

A wall of ransacked safe deposit boxes.

TROY GLOVER, 38 - a former boxer, chiseled visage, the kind of fighter who takes a licking and always gets himself up again - drills a precise hole into a lock, moves to the next. Troy is an American who's been in London since his teens and the type of guy you want on your side - loyal to a fault.

Working alongside him, in identical coveralls...

BARRY "COAL FACE" COULSON, 35 - a man-child, albeit one with a nasty upper cut and a face scarred from years of boxing - levers open the deposit boxes with a CROWBAR.

JIMMY "THE FIX" JOHNSON, 37 - the truly dangerous one here, all ego and simmering anger - scoops the contents into holdalls.

Troy checks his watch, signals to the others and they wrap up, moving with confident ease. Troy casts a final look around before moving out.

INT. GROUND FLOOR SERVICE CORRIDOR - NIGHT

A lift door is wedged open, granting access to the elevator shaft. Coal Face leans in, heaves on a rope and the holdalls emerge. He unties them and tosses them to...

Jimmy The Fix, who baskets them in a wheelie bin, adds a covering of paper waste, drags the wheelie bin towards the emergency exit, and slams his back against the release bar...

EXT. SIDE STREET, LONDON - NIGHT

Jimmy The Fix wheels the bin right up to the "East End Hygiene" Van and opens its back doors.

Quinlan watches in the rear mirror as Jimmy The Fix wedges the bin into place, jumps from the rear of the van.

The rear doors SLAM. Quinlan glances in the mirror, then over his left shoulder, towards the building's entrance, he feathers the accelerator and...

Jimmy MATERIALISES at Quinlan's open window, PRESSES the gun hard into Quinlan's temple. Quinlan revs the engine higher in surprise, then tries to lean away from the gun, his hands raised in fear of the weapon.

>   JIMMY THE FIX
> Stop revving the engine you pikey
> cretin. You'll wake the whole
> neighbourhood.

>   QUINLAN
> Put the gun away, gorger.

Jimmy enjoys Quinlan's raw terror.

>   JIMMY THE FIX
> You better be the fucking best
> driver. I'm talking Formula One.
> Because if you get me and my mates
> caught, I'll find you and kill you
> myself. You hear me, gyppo?

Finally, Jimmy The Fix lowers the gun, walks back towards the building. As he does, Quinlan GUNS the engine again.

>   JIMMY THE FIX (CONT'D)
> What the - ?

The van PEELS out - Jimmy The Fix pulls out his gun again.

>   JIMMY THE FIX (CONT'D)
> Stop the fucking van!

The van has to turn past Jimmy to get out of the alley.

>   JIMMY THE FIX (CONT'D)
> BASTARD! STOP!

Jimmy The Fix FIRES multiple SHOTS at Quinlan. The van veers, SLAMS into the wall. Comes to a rest.

Troy and Coal Face run out of the Exchange Building.

>   TROY
> Jesus. Jimmy!?

Jimmy The Fix holds the smoking gun. Turns to his mates' incredulous looks.

>   JIMMY THE FIX
> He sold us out. Took off with our
> haul.

Coal Face looks into the driver's seat, blanches at the horrible sight of Quinlan's bleeding corpse.

>   COAL FACE
> He's dead.

                    JIMMY THE FIX
          Always with the obvious, Coal Face.

                    TROY
               (yelling)
          Why? Why kill him? We could've
          sorted it out later. Now his people
          won't stop 'til we're dead too.

                    JIMMY THE FIX
          Shouldn't have been working with
          the pikeys in the first place.
          Vermin.

                    TROY
          This was his tip. We had a deal.
          Now we're fucked.

                    JIMMY THE FIX
          You're the smart one. You figure a
          way out.

SIRENS sound in the distance.

                    COAL FACE
          We gotta go.

Jimmy HANDS the GUN to Coal Face, hauls out Quinlan's body
and dumps him unceremoniously by an overloaded dumpster.

Coal Face wipes away the worst of the blood from inside the
van with a rag. Jimmy stoops for a plastic bag, shakes out
its contents and holds the bag open to Coal Face, who drops
the gun and the rag inside.

The SIRENS are louder.

EXT. COUNTRY LANE - DAWN

A tranquil expanse of fields. The "East End Hygiene" van
comes into view, driving fast down the narrow, winding road.

INT. EAST END HYGIENE VAN - DAWN

Jimmy The Fix drives, concentrating on the road.

On the opposite side, Troy stares out of the passenger window
and stews, absently clocks a utility vehicle that pulls from
a side road and falls in behind them.

In the middle seat, Coal Face bites his bottom lip. Troy
growls as Jimmy changes gears with a CRUNCH.

They come up on a slow, black Land Rover, and enter an
underpass. The sudden blackness matches their mood.

Exiting the tunnel...

A DEAD HORSE falls from above, landing on the hood with a giant CRASH.

Jimmy The Fix instinctively swerves, losing control of the van which CRASHES into the verge.

EXT. COUNTRY LANE - DAWN

The Land Rover and utility vehicle pull across the road, blocking the van front and back - not that it's going anywhere with a dead horse on its hood.

A horde of angry PIKEYS, life hardened, feral, line the bridge, stream from the vehicles, encircle the van, their shotguns raised waiting as...

ALBERT HEARN, 60, long white hair, true regal bearing - King of the Gypsies - emerges from the Black Land Rover, takes position opposite the van.

By his side, CHAS MCGREGOR,55 , a tough man who wants respect, but only knows how to fight his way to it.

On Albert's other flank stands his son, MANFRI HEARN, 33, wise beyond his years. Right now, his face is distraught - his eyes red, hate brewing within.

Albert raises his shotgun.

                    ALBERT
          Which one of you gorgers killed my
          boy?

INT. EAST END HYGIENE VAN - DAWN

Troy, Coal Face, and even Jimmy look at each other, terrified. Jimmy pulls the gun from the plastic bag. Troy stops him.

                    TROY
          Put that away. Let me do the talking.
             (loud, to Albert)
          I'm coming out.

Troy slowly opens the passenger door, steps outside.

EXT. COUNTRY LANE - DAWN

Troy raises his hands in the air. A dozen shot guns are aimed at him.

                    TROY
          We fucked up.

                    ALBERT
          For the last time.

                    TROY
          The cops came. We tried to get out
          of there. One of them got in the
          way of the van. Your son was
          driving. And they shot him. Nothing
          any of us could do. We're lucky we
          got out of there.

                    ALBERT
          The news says one of you shot him.

Jimmy The Fix steps out as well, hands also in the air.

                    JIMMY THE FIX
          You know the Old Bill - never miss
          a chance to lie - pin their fuck up
          on us.

Albert motions to his son, Manfri, and Chas, who both grab Troy, strong arm him towards the underpass.

Chas next pulls out a cowering Coal Face, throws him down, then inspects the inside of the van.

Beneath the bridge, shotguns inches from his face, Troy watches as Jimmy and Coal Face are dragged towards him too.

                    TROY
          We'd do anything to make it right.

                    MANFRI
          Nothing will bring my brother back.

Albert slams his fist into Troy's midriff, doubling him over, then signals up to the bridge and three nooses are dropped.

Still winded, Troy realises too late as the first noose is slipped over his head.

Coal Face panics, tries to scrabble away, and is rewarded with a broken nose as a gun butt smashes his face.

Jimmy the Fix resists but is quickly overcome. He refuses to show fear as the rope tightens around his neck.

Chas emerges from the van.

                    CHAS
          The fucking van's empty. You didn't
          get anything?

                    TROY
          We did. It's safely stashed.

Albert looks to Manfri, who shrugs - do they believe him?

CHAS
Just do them.

Chas signals up to the bridge. An engine revs and the ropes tighten, the men stand on tip toes.

TROY
(desperate)
You're right - we can't bring him back. But we can pay a tribute in his memory. It's all yours.

ALBERT
If we let you live?

TROY
(nods)
We'll take your word on that.

JIMMY THE FIX
All of it? Fuck no.

TROY
Shut up Jimmy. Yes, all.

Albert motions for Chas and Manfri to join him a few paces away. They talk quietly, out of earshot:

CHAS
We should just kill them all.

MANFRI
What if he's telling the truth?

CHAS
One way or another, they're responsible.

MANFRI
You'd start a war? Where would it end? Plus there's the take.

Albert nods, but Chas stews, unhappy. Albert returns to Troy and the others. He sizes them up. Then he slips the noose off Troy's neck, holds out his hand.

ALBERT
You have my word.

Troy nods, and they shake on it.

TROY
I'll draw you a map to the goods.

Albert nods. Jimmy The Fix and Chas eye each other warily.

CUT TO:

Blue Rev. (06/02/17)   7.

EXT. ANOTHER COUNTRY LANE - DAY

Troy, Jimmy The Fix, and Coal Face walk solemnly down the lane.

               JIMMY THE FIX
          All of it? Why'd you give him all
          of it?

               TROY
          This is your mess, Jimmy. You
          killed a man. You should be happy
          you're still alive.

               JIMMY THE FIX
          I say we man up, go take it back.

               COAL FACE
               (looking skyward)
          Jesus, what next?

     JIMMY THE FIX   RAY
I just told you what's next!   There is no next! There's no
We fucking...   we!

               TROY
          I'm out. I've had it with you. You
          and your temper are beyond help.

               JIMMY THE FIX
          Yeah? You can fuck off. We don't
          need your fucking help.

               COAL FACE
          I'm out too.

               JIMMY THE FIX
          No guts. Either of you. I don't
          need you no more.

Jimmy The Fix stops in tracks. Troy taps his head.

               TROY
          You need somebody's help.

Troy and Coal Face walk on, leaving Jimmy The Fix fuming, alone.

                                              CUT TO:

INT. LIVING ROOM, HILLCREST VIEW - EVENING

Sunday clutter, newspapers are strewn across the room, their headlines dominated by the Metal Exchange and Deposit heist.

In the background, we can hear the intermittent WHIR of an automatic screwdriver.

BEN "SPIDER" GLOVER, 14 - handsome, strong, but also a gawky teenager with the naive cockiness borne of hormones - is sprawled at Troy's feet, engrossed in a hand-held video game.

Troy taps Spider's feet:

          TROY
Bins.

          SPIDER
     (Eyes glued to his screen)
Yeah, yeah, just finish this...

          TROY
Now.

Spider grudgingly puts down his console, exits. Troy fumbles with the remotes, landing on a MUTED news broadcast, the name plate for the METAL EXCHANGE AND DEPOSIT in the top corner of the screen.

In the background, the screwdriver is replaced by the clanking of a small hammer on metal.

ON THE SCREEN

A dated photo of Quinlan fills the screen. Text appears on the screen: GYPSY HEIST.

Troy shakes his head at the screen, GROWLS as he battles the remote in search of sound.

A hand reaches around Troy, confiscates the remote and the screen goes blank. Troy turns around to face...

TANYA GLOVER, 38, - a tomboy, but hard edges softened by motherhood - armed with an automatic screw-driver and the inner workings of a fridge-freezer.

          TANYA
It's done. Forget Jimmy. He was only ever going to drag you down.

          TROY
But damn - what a haul, life would have been a lot easier.

          TANYA
It's not worth it Troy. The kids need their father. We can still take on the world...
     (holding the freezer motor)
A fridge at a time if we have to.

Troy smiles.

                             TROY
                   I could go back to boxing.

Tanya grabs Troy's cheek firmly.

                             TANYA
                   I've still got to look at you. I'm
                   not sure this could take another
                   beating.

Tanya kisses him. They hear the LAUGHTER of two young girls from down the hall.

EXT. JIMMY'S HOUSE - EVENING

Jimmy The Fix exits his more extravagant, newly constructed house. But right now he looks concerned. He stops on the walkway: hears a SCUFFLE through the hedge.

Jimmy The Fix bolts through the gate to see:

His son, LENNY JOHNSON, 14 - Jimmy's lumbering build, a viper's nest of faulty wiring in his head - beating the crap out of another TEEN BOY, who falls to the ground.

                             JIMMY THE FIX
                   I left the two of you playing video
                   games?

Lenny kicks him in the stomach.

                             LENNY
                   He was slagging Alicia. Said she
                   was a whore.

                             JIMMY THE FIX
                   Did he, now?

Jimmy The Fix looks at the writhing victim.

                             JIMMY THE FIX (CONT'D)
                   You don't kick him in the stomach,
                   you get him in the back of the head.
                       (motions to Lenny)
                   Go on, then.

Lenny smiles, delivers two powerful kicks to the boy's head.

                             JIMMY THE FIX (CONT'D)
                   That's right. You look after your
                   sister. Since your mother passed,
                   it's up to us men, eh?

Lenny nods.

                             JIMMY THE FIX (CONT'D)
                   Where is Alicia?

INT. LIVING ROOM, HILLCREST VIEW - EVENING

TWO GIRLS burst in, breathless and excitable, BFFs ERIN GLOVER, 10, and ALICIA JOHNSON, 10 - two flowers in bloom, so similar in appearance, they could be sisters.

Troy and Tanya watch, amused, as the excited girls bombard them with requests:

    ERIN   ALICIA
Daddy, can Alicia sleep over We're gonna do a fashion
tonight?   show.

      TROY
  Whoa, slow down there.
    (to Alicia)
  Alicia, does your dad even know
  you're here?

      ALICIA
    (confused)
  I'm here all the time.

      TANYA
  Tonight's not good honey.

Erin pouts.

      TROY
  Tell you what: why don't you two
  have a big bowl of ice cream and
  then we need to have a chat with
  the two of you.

      ERIN
  Dad!

      TROY
  Ice cream!

He points them to the kitchen. They run out of the room.

Troy's smile drops, pained at the thought of the coming conversation.

      TROY (CONT'D)
  Separating them is going to break
  their hearts.

      TANYA
  And what about you?

      TROY
  For sure. I don't want to put
  either of them through it.

She's watching closely now, treading carefully.

                    TANYA
          I'm talking about you. How are *you*
          going to cope without Alicia here?

                    TROY
          The same as you, she's part of the
          furniture. And to think she's got
          to live with Jimmy and that lout
          Lenny.

                    TANYA
          The way you look at her sometimes...

                    TROY
          Look at her how? What are you
          getting at woman?

                    TANYA
          As if she were yours. Not Jimmy's.
          I'm not accusing you...

Waiting for a denial that doesn't come.

                    TANYA (CONT'D)
          Troy?

Beat. Troy takes a deep breath.

                    TANYA (CONT'D)
          Oh Jesus.

Tanya recoils.

                    TROY
          Honestly? I don't know. It was just
          the once. You've got to remember,
          before Erin... there was a period
          when you and I thought we were
          through.

                    TANYA
          Does Jimmy know?

From outside comes the sound of REVVING MOPEDS.

EXT. HILLCREST VIEW - EVENING

Deepest suburbia, tended lawns, bins line the street awaiting
the next day's collection. Spider drags a bin to the end of
the driveway.

ACROSS THE STREET

Three Gypsy teens on Mopeds watch him: CASANOVA KELLY, 16,
possessive, brooding, several punches past handsome; BRENDEN
DOYLE 16, lumbering, strong, tends to be a follower, not a
leader; and BILLY BOSWELL, 17, fast-talking, smart aleck.

                    CASANOVA
          That's his house.

                    BRENDEN
          That's his son then?

                    CASANOVA
          Aye. Let's teach that son of bitch
          a lesson.

                    BILLY
          In memory of uncle Quin!

They get off their Mopeds, approach Spider, who can sense
trouble, but doesn't back down.

EXT. JIMMY'S GARDEN - EVENING

Lush, secluded. Jimmy The Fix stokes the coals of a high-end
BBQ grill with a hot poker, as GUESTS enjoy his food and
drink.

Coal Face, sporting his own black eye, helps Jimmy The Fix
flip big, juicy steaks.

                    JIMMY THE FIX
          I'm glad you came, Coal Face.

                    COAL FACE
          Your man didn't leave me much
          choice.

Coal Face looks warily across at ROMAN, 35, war ravaged, his
moral compass obliterated.

                    JIMMY THE FIX
          Good to hear. With his experience
          he doesn't come cheap.

                    COAL FACE
          He sucker punched me.

                    JIMMY THE FIX
          You weren't returning my calls.

Coal Face says nothing.

                    JIMMY THE FIX (CONT'D)
          I need you back running the gym.

                    COAL FACE
          Out means out.

Jimmy The Fix nods to another guest, DCI TONY FORDHAM, 37,
in street clothes, enjoying a drink with a couple of very
attractive YOUNG LADIES.

                    JIMMY THE FIX
          Remember him?

                    COAL FACE
          Fordham? Of course I remember! I
          haven't been punched that many
          times. We were boxing way back
          when... before you even started.

                    JIMMY THE FIX
          Right, and you know he's a
          Detective Chief Inspector now?

                    COAL FACE
          Yeah.

                    JIMMY THE FIX
          Well guess what he's investigating?

Coal Face looks at Jimmy the Fix - no way. Jimmy nods.

                    COAL FACE
          And you invited him here?

Jimmy hands Coal Face an envelope. Coal Face casts a
quizzical look, opens the envelope and pulls out...

A PHOTOGRAPH OF the gun that killed Quinlan and another of
the bloodied rag.

                    COAL FACE (CONT'D)
          I'm not with you. You're giving him
          evidence that ties you to his
          investigation?

                    JIMMY THE FIX
          No, not me! It's your finger prints
          on the gun, the rag that you used
          to mop up his blood...

Coal Face nibbles at his thumbnail as the implications
settle.

                    JIMMY THE FIX (CONT'D)
          ...it's probably still under your
          nails.

Coal Face drops his thumb.

                    COAL FACE
          You wouldn't?

Jimmy The Fix smiles as DCI Fordham approaches.

                    JIMMY THE FIX
          You want to risk it?

Coal Face shoves the photographs in his pocket.

					JIMMY THE FIX (CONT'D)
				You can keep those.

					DCI FORDHAM
				So why am I here Jimmy? What is
				you have to show me?

If Jimmy is offended by DCI's bluntness, it doesn't show.

					JIMMY THE FIX
				We were just reminiscing about
				O'Keefe's. You remember Coal Face?
				He's managing the place for me now.

					DCI FORDHAM
					(disinterested)
				Is that right?

Jimmy the Fix looks to Coal Face who reluctantly nods his agreement.

EXT. HILLCREST VIEW - EVENING

Spider gets in a few wild punches as the three Gypsy boys set upon him, but he's outgunned and soon on the receiving end of a harsh beating.

Then Troy CHARGES from the house. The three teens scramble to their Mopeds and take off, gesturing offensively.

Spider scuttles towards the house with a bust lip and a badly swollen eye.

Troy looks to Tanya in the doorway:

					TROY
				He's needs to be able to defend
				himself. Those damn video games are
				making him soft.

Still shellshocked from Troy's earlier confession, Tanya musters a helpless shrug of resignation.

					TANYA
				Okay fine. If it's what he wants.
					(beat)
				Just promise me one thing: he's
				never going to fight for money.

Troy looks to Spider. They both nod.

EXT. GARDEN - EVENING

Jimmy the Fix and DCI Fordham stand a discreet distance from the others.

Jimmy watches patiently as DCI Fordham shuffles through a
small wad of photographs, slots them back into an envelope,
his face a mask.

                    DCI FORDHAM
          Two hookers. So what? Who cares?

                    JIMMY THE FIX
          If you weren't in the Force, maybe
          nobody. But, unfortunately, they
          were both underage.

                    DCI FORDHAM
          No, that's not possible.

                    JIMMY THE FIX
          Trust me, it is. Could be really
          bad for you.

DCI Fordham moves closer to Jimmy the Fix, shoves the photos
at Jimmy's chest.

                    DCI FORDHAM
          So, what is this? A threat?

                    JIMMY THE FIX
          A threat? Come on! We grew up
          together didn't we? I'm trying to
          protect you.

                    DCI FORDHAM
          It's the same thing.

                    JIMMY THE FIX
          Not if it stays between us friends.

                    DCI FORDHAM
          And what do you want in return?

                    JIMMY THE FIX
              (dismissive)
          I'm not thinking about that. We can
          have a conversation when the time's
          right.

Jimmy smiles as DCI Fordham glares at Jimmy, then walks away.

INT. TROY'S GARAGE - DAY

Troy and Spider eagerly cut open two large cardboard boxes.
Inside one is a punching bag. Inside the other - boxing
gloves, and a collection of trophies, belts, and photos.

Troy chains the bag up to the ceiling as Spider looks through
the mementos of his father's boxing career.

                    SPIDER
          Why'd you leave America?

                    TROY
          I crossed the wrong people.

                    SPIDER
          Why?

                    TROY
          I thought I knew everything. I was
          wrong.

                    SPIDER
          Do you regret it?

                    TROY
          Well, I can never go back, but on
          the other hand, I'm here with you
          so...

Spider pulls out an old framed photograph of four smiling
young BOXERS, 20, standing in a row, arms around each other's
shoulders. Their signatures are scrawled at the bottom. We
recognise all four of the boxers:

TROY GLOVER...JIMMY JOHNSON...BARRY "COAL FACE"
COULSON...TONY FORDHAM.

                    SPIDER
          So were you the best of this lot?

                    TROY
          I held my own.

                    SPIDER
          So why'd you quit?

                    TROY
          To make it work, takes more than I
          was prepared to give. Then I met
          your mother and found better ways
          to make a living.

                    SPIDER
          Like what?

                    TROY
          Enough with the questions already.
          Get those gloves on and let's see
          what you've got.

Spider nods eagerly, laces up the gloves.

TRAINING MONTAGE

- Troy shows Spider how to work the bag.

- Spider jumps rope.

- Spider spars with Troy in the garage. Troy quickly breaks his son's defence. Motions for him to try again.

- TIME-LAPSE of SUNSETS and SUNRISE over the suburban house.

- As we watch, Spider keeps working the bag, and sprouts up before our eyes. He grows from the gawky boy, into the full frame worthy of a powerful fighter.

- He destroys the old bag with vicious lefts and rights. It falls from the ceiling in a cloud of plaster and dust.

INT. BOXING CLUB - DAY

Held together with gaffer tape and memories. The walls plastered with photos of past fighters.

Spider, now 21, has become a sculpted Rottweiler. He seeks out Coal Face, leaning against the ring.

          SPIDER
  Thanks for this opportunity, Mr.
  Coulson.

         COAL FACE
  First off, everyone calls me Coal
  Face. Second, Your dad knows you're
  here?

          SPIDER
  Oh come on. I don't have to ask his
  permission anymore.

Coal Face doesn't like this answer.

        SPIDER (CONT'D)
  Yes. He knows. My mother doesn't.

Coal Face nods, knowingly.

        SPIDER (CONT'D)
  Dad says you were like family.
  You've trained the best.

Coal Face hesitates, then:

         COAL FACE
  All right, enough... this is the
  way this is going to go.

On the wall nearby is the same framed photos of the four young boxers: Troy, Coal Face, Jimmy The Fix and Fordham.

CONTINUE TRAINING MONTAGE:

- Spider works out in the ring with Coal Face.

- Spider spars, he's quick and powerful. Coal Face can't hide his admiration.

- Spider pumps iron in the training room.

INT. CHANGING ROOM, WORKING MEN'S CLUB - NIGHT

Rudimentary, old school, and bustling with BOXERS huddled in their respective CAMPS readying themselves for battle.

We hear the background SOUND of a fight in progress.

A fight night promotion poster on the wall screams: "29 SEPTEMBER 2017. Promoted by JOHNSON PROMOTIONS. BEN SPIDER GLOVER v LOCOMOTIVE JONES" takes second billing.

In the corner, Spider sits on a bench in boxing shorts. Coal Face squats in front of Spider wrapping his knuckles.

EXT. WORKING MEN'S CLUB - NIGHT

A gathering crowd of thick-necked hard MEN in tight suits, their WOMEN an assault on the ozone layer, fake tans, tits and teeth.

A battered hatchback pulls up, "GLOVER'S LOCKSMITHS" on the side, innocuous amongst the pimped up rides and tinted windows lining the street.

INT. HATCHBACK - NIGHT

Troy, slightly aged, unbuckles his seat-belt, glances at Tanya who glares out of the window at the front of the Working Men's Club. Troy fixes a smile on his face, twists to the rear of the car.

     TROY
  Okay kiddo, any spare hugs back
  there?

Erin, now 16 - a beautiful young woman with cascading hair, a discreet peace symbol tattoo on the side of her neck - sits in the rear.

     ERIN
   (To Troy)
  One last time. Ask her. Please!

Troy glances quickly at Tanya, who turns to look at Erin:

                         TANYA
               No! You're not going in. End of
               discussion.

Troy shrugs at Erin apologetically and plants a kiss on her
cheek. Erin slaps a slim gift box in his hand.

                         ERIN
               Give it to him before the fight,
               okay?

                         TROY
               Got it.

A final glance back to Tanya, a speculative half smile:

                         TROY (CONT'D)
               Let him get this out of his system.
               If I tried to stop him, he'd just
               do it anyway, without telling us.
               It's much better this way.

Tanya shakes her head, her eyes fixed in front.

                         TANYA
               It's just more of the same from
               you...

Troy falls silent - he knows there's no winning this
argument. He eases himself out of the car.

EXT. WORKING MEN'S CLUB - NIGHT

Troy watches the car pull away, lets loose a resigned SIGH,
before he joins the CROWD heading inside to...

INT. WORKING MEN'S CLUB - NIGHT

A grand space maintained on a limited budget. The same fight
night promotion poster on the wall.

Troy, conspicuous in work-wear, weaves his way through the
CROWD, nodding to a couple of familiar faces, he comes face
to face with...

JIMMY THE FIX

Sharply dressed in stark contrast to Troy. Nearby is Lenny,
now also 21, who's turned into a fully grown dark malignancy.
Alicia, now 16, stands at her brother's shoulder, dressed up,
but sullen, like she'd rather be anywhere else. She still
looks like Erin's sister.

Jimmy's looks Troy up and down, smiles.

JIMMY THE FIX
Troy. It's been a while.

TROY
Jimmy.

JIMMY THE FIX
(disingenuous)
You're looking well. The key-cutting business must be good?
(gesturing around)
What do you think? Good turn out?

Troy glances over Jimmy's shoulder towards the changing room, remains silent.

JIMMY THE FIX (CONT'D)
Well anyway. We're counting on your boy tonight.

Troy smiles tightly and moves on, ending further conversation.

INT. CHANGING ROOM, WORKING MEN'S CLUB - NIGHT

Through the bustle, Spider catches glimpses of LOCOMOTIVE JONES (30's) - a barbarous, hulking mass - loosening his neck and shoulders, listening to whispered instructions from his TRAINER.

Troy pushes through the crowd to Spider. A parent's smile of pride, tinged with anxiety:

TROY
So Jimmy's counting on you?

SPIDER
(shrugs)
Well yeah, he's the promoter so...

Troy moves Spider a couple of paces away, the closest to privacy he'll get. Studies Spider, looking for a tell.

SPIDER (CONT'D)
What?

TROY
Watch out is all...

SPIDER
(interrupting)
No more lectures, okay?

TROY
I just don't want you making the same mistakes I made.

                    SPIDER
          I got it. I understand.

The bell RINGS.

                    TROY
          Okay, look. I didn't come to argue.
          Here...

Troy hands the gift box to Spider, who clumsily opens it to
REVEAL a gold chain with a pendant, FOUR BOXING GLOVES in the
shape of a four leaf clover.

                    TROY (CONT'D)
          It's a Four Leaf Glover.

Spider smiles.

                    BOXING ANNOUNCER (O.S.)
          Bout two, Jones and Glover, three
          minutes.

Locomotive Jones barges past Spider, heading into the ring.

                    SPIDER
          Thanks dad.

Spider holds his hands out to his dad as Coal Face shepherds
Spider away.

                    COAL FACE
          Move it, come on.

                    TROY
          Son?

Spider looks back.

                    TROY (CONT'D)
               (encouraging)
          Don't drop your left.

Spider smiles, nods, as he and Coal Face move out of Troy's
earshot.

                    COAL FACE
               (to Spider, surprised)
          So he doesn't know about Jimmy?

Spider's face is set in a grim line.

INT. RINGSIDE, WORKING MEN'S CLUB - NIGHT

Troy hustles through the crowd, takes his seat to the rear.

The bell RINGS.

IN THE RING

Locomotive Jones bolts forward and catches Spider behind the ear, follows up with a wild haymaker.

Spider feints and counters with a succession of jabs and the fight settles.

The BELL ends the round.

RINGSIDE

Troy scans the crowd and spots Jimmy holding court to the PATRONS around him. Lenny and Alicia sit on either side of him.

BACK TO THE RING

The BELL RINGS again. Locomotive Jones trudges around the ring, is made to look clumsy by Spider, finally wrapping his arms around Spider's neck.

SPIDER'S POV

To the rear, Troy hollers his support.

Jimmy showboats for the other patrons, pays no regard to the fight.

LOCOMOTIVE JONES

Catches Spider with a low shot.

Spider LOSES IT - unleashes a brutal combination of punches, ending the fight with a devastating uppercut to Jones' jaw.

Now he's got Jimmy's attention. Jimmy glares up at Spider who glares back with a look that says, "how'd you like those apples?"

The referee counts down as Jimmy, angry, makes a swift exit.

INT. CHANGING ROOM, WORKING MEN'S CLUB - NIGHT

Spider tosses his gloves on to the bench. Coal Face, nervous, moves as fast as he can to remove the tape.

     COAL FACE
  Didn't he say he'd see you right
  next time? He's your manager - he's
  looking out for you.

                        SPIDER
              Fuck that, he's looking out for
              himself.

                        JIMMY THE FIX (O.S.)
              Troy was always bleating that I
              lost control too quickly...

Coal Face recoils. Spider turns to...

Jimmy the Fix, flanked by an entourage of FIVE BODYGUARDS,
including Roman - all heavily muscled.

                        JIMMY THE FIX (CONT'D)
              Right now? It's taking everything
              I've got, not to lose it with you.

Spider stands defiant.

                        JIMMY THE FIX (CONT'D)
              You realise you've let down some
              very important people? Your winning
              has put me in a very difficult
              position.

                        SPIDER
              Yeah, important to who? Because
              those important to me would be let
              down if I lost.

                        JIMMY THE FIX
              I am the ONLY person important to
              you right now!

                        SPIDER
              And you should be helping me take
              on the world, not take a fucking
              dive.

Jimmy's mouth twitches.

                        JIMMY THE FIX
              Jesus, you sound like your father.

On Jimmy's signal, a bodyguard grabs for Spider. Spider
floors him with a punch.

                        SPIDER
              And I should have listened to him.

                        JIMMY THE FIX
              Kid. Trust me, I've seen hundreds
              of fighters come through here.
              You're not that good. And I've got
              a piece of paper that says I own
              you and you'll do what I say.

                    SPIDER
          Yeah? Or what?

                    JIMMY THE FIX
          Or your pretty little sister will
          end up looking like Coal Face.

Spider goes for Jimmy The Fix, which is signal enough for
Roman and the other bodyguards to mete out a beating.

INT. HATCHBACK - NIGHT

Tanya and Erin look across to the Working Men's Club,
concerned and bored respectively.

Jimmy The Fix, Lenny, and Alicia exit as a Land Rover pulls
up outside.

Erin waves.

                    ERIN
          Alicia!

Alicia nods coldly in Erin's direction, climbs into the Land
Rover and it pulls away. Erin looks disappointed.

Tanya returns her worried look to the club. Where are her son
and husband?

INT. CHANGING ROOM, WORKING MEN'S CLUB - NIGHT

Troy enters, smiling, looking for Spider.

He sees Coal Face, crouched in the corner ministering to a
prostate body. Troy knows immediately who it is. He jumps
over the bench.

                    COAL FACE
          His arm's broken, maybe a couple of
          ribs.

Troy pushes Coal Face aside and tends to Spider's battered
body.

                    TROY
          This was Jimmy right? You were
          supposed to be looking out for him!

                    COAL FACE
          I called an ambulance.

Troy springs towards Coal Face, pushes him against the
lockers.

                    TROY
          What have you got him into?

                    COAL FACE
          Me? It was Spider's decision, he
          wanted the fight and *you* knew Jimmy
          was promoting it.

                    TROY
          But not counting on him losing.

Spider slowly opens his swollen left eye.

                    SPIDER
          Sorry dad... I should've
          listened...

                    TROY
          Shh... it's okay.

Troy coaxes Spider to his feet, brushing past Coal Face.

                    TROY (CONT'D)
              (to Coal Face)
          Don't think that this is over.

INT. HOSPITAL ROOM - NIGHT

Modern, whitewashed sterility. Spider is propped up in bed, his face swollen and badly bruised, his wrist in a cast.

Troy approaches with Tanya and Erin.

                    SPIDER
          Sorry mum, you were right...

Tanya starts fussing over Spider.

                    TANYA
          Promise me - no more of this,
          alright? Promise!

Spider nods, but exchanges a worried look with Troy.

INT. ALBERT'S TRAILER - NIGHT

A chintz monstrosity of gold, mirrors, cherubs and boxing gloves. Walls adorned with old photos of Albert as a younger man in various boxing poses. "King of the Gypsies" logos splashed liberally around.

Albert rests in bed. He looks pale and frail.

At his bedside sits Chas McGregor, showing Albert an old PHOTOGRAPH of them together as younger men, both beaten to a pulp, but smiling.

                    CHAS
          Those were the days Albert, weren't
          they?

SANDRA, 40, Manfri's wife and a walking fire hazard of nylon
and hairspray, wrings out a cloth in the sink, gives it to
the curvaceous young beauty, and Chas' daughter, CASSIE
MCGREGOR, 20, who mops Albert's forehead with it.

Manfri enters, and stops, surprised to see Chas. Sandra
throws her arms around Manfri's neck and plants a smacker of
a kiss on his lips. Manfri grins and grabs her bum playfully
in a very public display of affection.

                    SANDRA
          Chas and Cassie came over to spend
          some time with Albert. That's kind,
          isn't it?

Manfri doesn't nod. Chas rises.

                    CHAS
          I'll leave you lovebirds to it.

He bends down to Albert, clenches his fist.

                    CHAS (CONT'D)
          You keep fighting, you hear me?

He gives Albert a wink, then SNAPS HIS FINGERS at Cassie, and
they leave. Manfri, worried, sits at Albert's bed, feels his
forehead, then looks at Sandra.

                    MANFRI
          No change?

                    SANDRA
              (shakes her head)
          Stubborn bastard still refuses to
          go to hospital.

                    ALBERT
          I'll die in my own bed, not some
          gorger hospital.

                    MANFRI
          Pipe down you or we'll put you out
          of your misery ourselves.

Manfri puts the old picture back in place on the wall.

                    MANFRI (CONT'D)
          What did Chas want?

Sandra rolls her eyes.

SANDRA
Same old story. He was practically
drooling. Like it's his coronation.

MANFRI
Any chance this will all get
settled peacefully?

Sandra shakes her head, no.

ALBERT
(wheezing)
Chas only knows fighting...

Albert is consumed by a hacking, phlegm-filled COUGH.

EXT. THE FIX - NIGHT

Troy enters past the DOORMAN at the entrance to this typical
seedy strip club.

INT. THE FIX - NIGHT

Darkness and neon try their best to hide the cheap plastic
decor. Troy navigates past scantily clad GIRLS flitting
between pot bellied SUITS and rough LOCALS. He reaches a
heavy metal door at the back...

The BOUNCER looks Troy up and down, then the CLICK of a
MAGNETIC LOCK allows Troy through to...

INT. REAR CORRIDOR, THE FIX - NIGHT

A service corridor, painted floor and walls heavily scuffed.
A FROSTED WINDOW on one wall, a large wooden door on the
other. Troy pushes into...

INT. REAR OFFICE, THE FIX - NIGHT

Decorated like a private club room: wood panel walls, thick
carpet, mahogany desk and wing-back chairs.

Roman sits in one of the chairs, Lenny in another, and
between them, Jimmy The Fix, holding court over a bottle of
whisky.

Troy wastes no time:

TROY
You stay the fuck away from my
family! You hear?

                    JIMMY THE FIX
               You don't get to come in here
               bloody barking at me... not
               anymore.

Roman and Lenny stand, tense, on guard. Troy stays focussed on Jimmy The Fix:

                    TROY
               You go near my family, I'll do more
               than bark!

                    JIMMY THE FIX
               Is that a threat?

Troy catches the first hint of Jimmy's mouth twitch...

                    TROY
                  (backing off a bit)
               I'm just looking out for my family.

Troy picks up a framed picture of Alicia from Jimmy's desk.

                    TROY (CONT'D)
               You of all people should understand
               that.

Beat.

Jimmy The Fix struts to a large safe at the back of the room, and makes a big theatrical show of opening it. He purposely lets Troy see inside: stacked notes, bags of coins, folders and ledgers.

Jimmy The Fix rifles through the folders, and pulls out one, throws it across the desk to Troy, who picks it up slowly, opens it to REVEAL...

PHOTOGRAPHS chronicle the past 7 years of Troy's and Tanya's life in decline: downsizing, a crappy house, a crappier car, Spider boxing, Erin blossoming.

                    JIMMY THE FIX
               I particularly like that one.

Jimmy The Fix points to a photograph, taken from the street, that shows Erin, semi-naked in her bedroom.

                    JIMMY THE FIX (CONT'D)
               If she ever wants to work here...

Lenny LAUGHS.

Troy SMASHES his fist down on the desk, makes a move towards Jimmy. He is grabbed by Roman and Lenny, manhandled towards the door.

                    TROY
          You stay the fuck away.

Jimmy The Fix smiles...

                    JIMMY THE FIX
          I should thank you.

Troy just keeps struggling.

                    JIMMY THE FIX (CONT'D)
          Quitting when you did. It was like
          you released the handbrake and...

Jimmy The Fix indicates differing trajectories with the flat
of his hands. He considers Troy's to be in steep decline.

                    TROY
              (motions to the folder)
          But you can't quite get past it can
          you? And controlling Spider to get
          to me? It's time to move on Jimmy.
          Don't you think?

Troy pulls his arms free - it's time to leave but he can do
it on his own.

                    JIMMY THE FIX
          You're right. And I'll tell you
          what? If you want your boy out so
          badly...

Troy stops at the doorway, looks back at Jimmy The Fix who
drops the folder back into the safe.

                    JIMMY THE FIX (CONT'D)
          Lenny could do with your help on a
          small job.

Lenny smiles at Troy - the same crooked smile as his father.
Jimmy The Fix waves a piece of paper at Troy, enticing.

                    JIMMY THE FIX (CONT'D)
          I'll tear this up.

                    TROY
          And if I don't?

Jimmy shrugs - a contract's a contract.

                    TROY (CONT'D)
          There's some other way. You know
          I'm out of that line of work.

                    JIMMY THE FIX
          I want you. You were the best.
          Teach my boy here the ropes.

Beat.

                    TROY
          Deal - but no guns.

Satisfied, Jimmy The Fix nods and downs his whisky.

INT. MARQUEE TENT - DAY

Filled with MALE GYPSYS paying their respects, sitting around a casket that rests on a plinth in the centre.

Manfri sits next to the casket, his head bowed, just behind him sit two of the gypsies we met earlier outside Troy's house -- Brendan and Billy Boswell, now in their 20s.

Chas McGregor makes his through the crowd, accompanied by Casanova Kelly, now 22.

Chas McGregor parks himself next to Manfri, who doesn't even look up. Chas fidgets, moves ever closer to Manfri.

                    CHAS
          He was a good man Albert was. Kept
          the peace all these years.

Chas makes a little sign towards the heavens.

                    CHAS (CONT'D)
          He had a right hand that could drop
          a horse. I remember we were going
          at it...

                    MANFRI
          Now's not the time for this.

                    CHAS
              (ignoring him)
          ...Never seen rain like it, ankle
          deep in mud we were. Blood
          everywhere, cheeks so swollen we
          couldn't see. Dead on our feet,
          neither of us willing to back down.
          We had to be pulled apart, judged a
          draw. Can you imagine? Never a
          match like that to this day.
              (conspiratorial)
          ...And you know what he said?

                    MANFRI
          That it was time to move on?

                    CHAS
          I'll never forget it. He said he'd
          never known a tougher man. Mother's
          life...
                    (MORE)

                    CHAS (CONT'D)
          He said that if he died, God rest
          his soul, without losing his crown,
          that I'd be next in line. Do you
          see what I'm saying?

Beat.

                    CHAS (CONT'D)
          He never fought again after that...
          so by rights...

Chas pulls his shoulders back, REVEALS a gold chain with a pendant "KING OF THE GYPSIES".

                    MANFRI
          Nice necklace.

                    CHAS
             (proud)
          It was a present.

                    MANFRI
          And did you get earrings to match?

Chas jumps to his feet, chest puffed out, Manfri rises to fend him off... and the tenuous harmony disintegrates.

Throughout the tent, simmering tensions erupt, battle lines are drawn with FISTS.

At the centre of it all, Manfri and Chas battle in front of Albert's casket. But Manfri is no match for Chas, who fells him with a quick flurry of brutal punches.

Manfri falls back into the casket - CRASH! The casket hits the ground and the other fights peter out and stop.

Chas stands, panting for breath, but victorious. The self-proclaimed King of the Gypsies. He looks around for affirmation, but doesn't miss the looks of disapproval scattered around the room.

INT. BEDROOM, IVY COTTAGE - NIGHT

Cramped, shabby furniture. Troy rummages through a wardrobe, he comes up empty. He moves to the drawers and locates a small black pouch, throws it into a duffel bag, zips it up as the door to the room opens. Troy turns to:

Tanya, who blocks the doorway with a stern expression. Erin sticks her head in too.

                    ERIN
          Hey daddy.

                    TROY
          Hey honey.

Troy hoists the duffel bag onto his shoulder, squeezes by.

TROY (CONT'D)
Said I'd meet Coal Face at the gym.

TANYA
You forgot something.

Troy turns back to see A DRILL laid in the middle of the bed. He collects it and pushes past her again.

Tanya follows him, onto:

INT. THE LANDING, IVY COTTAGE - NIGHT

She stands at the top of the stairs as Troy reaches the front door.

TANYA (CONT'D)
Troy?

He opens the door.

TANYA (CONT'D)
I wouldn't bother coming back.

Troy hesitates, then exits.

ERIN
(high pitched)
Mom? What are you saying?

Erin, upset, scrambles down the stairs after her father.

EXT. IVY COTTAGE - NIGHT

An uninspiring terraced house, which renders it's name ironic.

ERIN
Daddy?

Troy drops the duffel bag, hugs her tight.

TROY
(gently)
I need to go, honey.

ERIN
But what Mom said...

TROY
I'll be back soon and then we'll work things out. Okay?

Erin nods her head, biting her bottom lip.

                         ERIN
              Promise?

                         TROY
              On my life.

Troy gives her his best smile, glances to the upstairs window from where Tanya looks back down. The curtain drops and with it, Troy's smile.

EXT. RESIDENTIAL STREET - NIGHT

A van pulls up across from a mansion in a posh neighbourhood.

INT. VAN - NIGHT

Inside, Coal Face is in the driver's seat. Troy glares at Lenny:

                         TROY
                   (contempt)
              This is your grand plan?

                         LENNY
              He's a banker.

                         TROY
              So that makes it okay, does it?

                         LENNY
              They're all a bunch of thieves.

Beat. Troy has no appetite for this.

                         TROY
              Fine. Let's get it over with.

He slides open the door of the van, and they get out.

EXT. RESIDENTIAL STREET - NIGHT

A dark sedan pulls to a stop in view of the van and banker's house, Roman at the wheel.

EXT. BANKER'S HOUSE - NIGHT

At the door, Coal Face hands Troy his tools.

Lenny hovers, jumpy. From inside his hoodie he pulls out a plastic bag we've seen before -- and takes out the gun.

Troy senses something and turns, snatches the gun from Lenny, shoves it into his pocket.

                    TROY
            I said no guns.

Lenny backs off hands in the air

                    LENNY
            All right bruv. Chill.

Lenny shoves the plastic bag into the back of his sloppy jeans, discreetly checks another handgun tucked in the waistband.

Troy drills the lock.

INT. DARK SEDAN - NIGHT

Roman watches as Troy, Coal Face and Lenny enter the house.

INT. BANKER'S HOUSE, MASTER BEDROOM - NIGHT

Spacious and well appointed. Working in the beam of Coal Face's torch, Troy drills a tiny hole in a wall safe.

Lenny flicks his torch across a gleaming dresser cluttered with perfume bottles, his fingers closing around his gun and moves closer to Troy.

A muffled THUD comes from somewhere in the house.

Coal Face nods towards the door and Lenny moves to investigate...

INT. BANKER'S HOUSE, SECOND BEDROOM - NIGHT

Lenny shines the torch around a mess of make-up and jewellery, photographs of a pretty girl tacked to the mirror.

He pockets some loose change from the dresser, rifles through drawers, holding first a bra, then a pair of panties out for size.

He explores a built-in wardrobe, brimming with clothes. He reaches down for a pair of tights amongst the laundry within, when the light of his torch lands on...

A GIRL, 15 - the one in the pictures - who hides in the corner.

Lenny YANKS her out, doesn't notice...

INSIDE THE WARDROBE

A mobile phone on the floor, its screen still bright from recent use.

INT. MASTER BEDROOM, BANKER'S HOUSE - NIGHT

Troy opens the safe to reveal jewellery and cash.

Troy glances sideways, looking for Lenny as Coal Face reaches for the jewels. Troy grabs Coal Face's arm, shoves him against the wall, his forearm to his throat.

>   COAL FACE
>   What you doing?

>   TROY
>   Why are you here? What's he got on
>   you?

>   COAL FACE
>   I'm broke, Troy. Not many
>   opportunities like this.

>   TROY
>   Tell me the truth!

Troy reaches for the drill, presses it to the underside of Coal Face's chin.

>   COAL FACE
>   Come on, this is Jimmy type of
>   shit, not you. Why does it matter
>   so much?

>   TROY
>   Because you dragged Spider into it.

Troy starts the drill, the tip pierces skin, draws blood.

>   COAL FACE
>   Jimmy can put me away. If he wants
>   to.

Troy relaxes the drill.

>   COAL FACE (CONT'D)
>   The gun that killed Quinlan?
>   Jimmy's gun? My prints are all over
>   it. And the rag. Jimmy's got them
>   both.

The walls are washed by STROBING BLUE LIGHTS. Troy releases Coal Face.

EXT. BANKER'S HOUSE - NIGHT

WPC MAXWELL, 24 - wet behind the ears, eager - ventures around the house, peering into the windows as...

Coal Face scurries to safety with the duffel bags.

INT. BANKER'S HOUSE, SECOND BEDROOM - NIGHT

Unaffected by the police lights.

Lenny's arm is around the girl's neck. He grinds his crotch against her butt, yanking at her night-shirt, its buttons popping as she tries to resist.

He takes the gun from his waistband, places it on the dresser.

> TROY (O.S.)
> The hell you doing? Can't you just burgle the place like a normal person?

> LENNY
> Just a bit of fun, bruv, innit?

> TROY
> This is nowhere near fun.

Troy grabs for Lenny who retreats around the bed, shielding himself behind the girl, swipes at Troy with a KNIFE.

THE DOORBELL RINGS... distracts Lenny for a split second, enough for Troy to LUNGE, pushing the girl to safety.

Troy grabs Lenny's wrist, forces him to drop the knife, then drags him from the room...

He misses Lenny SNATCH his GUN back as they pass the dresser.

INT. BANKER'S HOUSE, BACK ENTRANCE - NIGHT

Troy peers through a panel window - all clear. He opens the back door a fraction and shoves Lenny out...

EXT. BANKER'S HOUSE - NIGHT

...Into WPC Maxwell. She skids, crashing on to her backside. She skitters backwards like a crab.

WPC MAXWELL'S POV

Lenny raises his gun, the barrel pointing at WPC and... BOOM!

...Lenny's head EXPLODES in a red spray.

TROY

Holds the smoking GUN as Lenny falls to the ground dead... WPC Maxwell looks up at him wide eyed.

Coal Face drives off in the van.

Troy drops the gun, turns, and vaults over the fence, sprinting as fast as he can out of there.

INT. DARK SEDAN - NIGHT

Roman watches the van peel off down the street with only Coal Face inside, past the police car with flashing lights.

Roman pulls out after the van, flips open his phone to make a call.

EXT. COAL FACE'S STUDIO - NIGHT

Squalid. Coal Face staggers through the door with the duffel bags.

EXT. CITY STREET - NIGHT

Troy walks briskly, head down, mobile phone to his ear, approaching a bus stop, he jumps on a bus as its doors are about to close.

>   TROY
>   (into phone)
>   Coal Face... Call me back. If I
>   have to come over there I'll kill
>   you myself!

INT. COAL FACE'S STUDIO - NIGHT

Coal Face paces, fists clenching and unclenching.

A KNOCK at the door...

>   COAL FACE
>   Troy?

EXT. COAL FACE'S STUDIO - NIGHT

Troy knocks on the door. He pushes the door open into...

INT. COAL FACE'S STUDIO - NIGHT

Troy stares down at Coal Face, sprawled DEAD on the sofa, a bullet to the head.

Troy's phone VIBRATES. He answers:

>   TROY
>   (into mobile)
>   Jimmy... He tried to take out a
>   cop...

INT. REAR OFFICE, THE FIX - NIGHT

                    JIMMY THE FIX
              (into his mobile)
          I'm going to fucking rape your
          daughter, skin your wife. I'm going
          to burn your FUCKING HOUSE DOWN!!!

EXT. COAL FACE'S STUDIO - NIGHT

Troy is already on the run. He hangs up on Jimmy The Fix. Dials again:

                    TROY
              (into mobile)
          Spider, listen to me very
          carefully... hurry... get mom and
          Erin somewhere safe...

INT. HALLWAY, IVY COTTAGE - NIGHT

Spider, using his one wrist not in a cast, lugs a suitcase down the stairs where Tanya madly sorts through her purse.

                    TANYA
          How long are we going to be gone?

Spider glances at Tanya, peers up the stairs...

                    SPIDER
          I don't know. Dad says he's sorting
          it out.

INT. ERIN'S BEDROOM - NIGHT

A chaos of clothes. Erin contemplates which pair of shoes to add to her hastily packed case as...

Spider barges in, grabs a pair of shoes from her hand, tosses them into the case.

                    SPIDER
          Come on. We gotta go. Now!

INT. HALLWAY, IVY COTTAGE - NIGHT

Tanya waits at the doorway as Spider and Erin bundle down the stairs.

                    TANYA
          What does he mean, 'sorting it out?'

INT. INTERROGATION ROOM, POLICE STATION - NIGHT

Sparse. A two-way mirror and three bare walls. FLICKER of a fluorescent light, clicking HUM of an ageing AC.

DCI Fordham sits at a table across from Troy. He tears off a top sheet and considers the several pages of handwritten notes in front of him, leans back and contemplates Troy for a long beat.

> DCI FORDHAM
> Answers a lot of unanswered questions...

DCI Fordham goes back to the notes.

> DCI FORDHAM (CONT'D)
> ...And you say that Jimmy has the gun that killed Quinlan?

Troy nods.

> DCI FORDHAM (CONT'D)
> You saw it?

> TROY
> No. Coal Face told me.

DCI Fordham rubs his thumb and forefinger together, deep in thought.

> DCI FORDHAM
> In a court of law, all this could implicate Coal Face as much as Jimmy.

Troy knows where this is going.

> TROY
> I would be a witness.

DCI Fordham shakes his head sympathetically.

> DCI FORDHAM
> You're accused of murder yourself.

> TROY
> I saved a police officer.

> DCI FORDHAM
> Don't get me wrong, we can start building a case against him. I'm just saying be prepared. And maybe he'll incriminate himself up when I question him.

DCI Fordham gathers his papers, moving towards the door.

                    TROY
          We go back what? Twenty-five years?

                    DCI FORDHAM
          Something like that.

                    TROY
          I know we haven't always seen eye
          to eye.

                    DCI FORDHAM
          You ended up with Trisha fair and
          square. It's ancient history. I
          don't begrudge you that. But some
          of your life choices, maybe...

                    TROY
          I've left that life behind, trust
          me. And I want you to know, I'm
          trusting you with the most important
          thing in the world - my family.

                    DCI FORDHAM
              (nods)
          Whatever happens I'll see to it
          that they're safe.

INT. UNDERGROUND CAR PARK, POLICE STATION - NIGHT

Dark, secure. Tanya, Spider and Erin load their possessions
into an unmarked police car, watched over by TWO OFFICERS.

INT. INTERROGATION ROOM, POLICE STATION - NIGHT

The same room in which we saw Troy. This time, Jimmy the Fix
sits, distraught, at the same table, holding a photograph of
Troy in front of him.

                    JIMMY THE FIX
          Is this really necessary? Right
          now? You know who they are.

DCI Fordham taps his finger on the table.

                    DCI FORDHAM
          I'd appreciate it.

Beat.

                    JIMMY THE FIX
          Troy Glover...

DCI Fordham places a picture of Coal Face on the table.

                    JIMMY THE FIX (CONT'D)
          Coal Face.
               (correcting himself)
          Coulson. Barry Coulson.

DCI Fordham slides another picture towards him - it's Quinlan
Hearn, the gypsy Jimmy The Fix murdered in the original
heist. Jimmy picks it up.

                    JIMMY THE FIX (CONT'D)
          No idea. Who is it?

                    DCI FORDHAM
          You don't know him? A fucking
          pikey?

Jimmy's mouth twitches.

                    JIMMY THE FIX
          I don't see the connection.
               (points to Troy's picture)
          He kills my son and you're showing
          me pictures of some pikey that was
          killed seven fucking years...

Beat. Jimmy senses he's slipped up...

                    DCI FORDHAM
          Seven years is very specific. What
          do you know about it?

                    JIMMY THE FIX
               (recovering)
          It was in the news. You guys
          couldn't figure out who did it.

                    DCI FORDHAM
          You have a safe in your office?

                    JIMMY THE FIX
          Yeah, so?

                    DCI FORDHAM
          What if you and I went to go take a
          look inside together?

Jimmy The Fix glances around the room. His eyes settle on the
audio equipment.

                    JIMMY THE FIX
          You didn't press record.

                    DCI FORDHAM
          Did you kill Quinlan Hearn?

Jimmy leans forward angrily.

                    JIMMY THE FIX
          Enough with the games. I go down,
          you go down, remember? You can't
          touch me!

Fordham says nothing.

                    JIMMY THE FIX (CONT'D)
          I'll tell you what you're going to
          do. Go run your fucking tests on
          the gun that Troy used to blow my
          kid's head off. And you know what
          you're gonna find?

Fordham shakes his head. Jimmy The Fix picks up the photo of the dead Quinlan.

                    JIMMY THE FIX (CONT'D)
          That it's the same gun used to kill
          this low life Gypsy. And that's how
          you're going to send Troy to jail,
          where he's not going to last a
          week. Understand? Or else...

Fordham silently nods.

                    JIMMY THE FIX (CONT'D)
          Now where's my daughter? This
          fucking place...

INT. POLICE STATION, WAITING ROOM - NIGHT

A FAMILY LIAISON OFFICER (early 30's) - matronly, gentle - sits, clipboard in hand, alongside a glassy-eyed Alicia.

                    FAMILY LIAISON OFFICER
          ...and your mother? Have you
          spoken...

                    JIMMY THE FIX (O.S.)
          ...Her mother is dead!

The Family Liaison Officer and Alicia turn to see an irate Jimmy approach.

                    ALICIA
          She took the easy way out.

Jimmy the Fix ushers Alicia towards the exit.

                    FAMILY LIAISON OFFICER
          Mr Johnson... before you go, I had
          some concerns.

Jimmy the Fix turns on the Family Liaison Officer, who is joined by DCI Fordham.

                    JIMMY THE FIX
          Whatever it is, I'm not interested.

Jimmy's eyes lock on DCI Fordham.

                    JIMMY THE FIX (CONT'D)
          You've wasted enough of my time.

As Jimmy bundles her out, Alicia slips something into
Fordham's hand as she gives him a fleeting smile, vulnerable,
her eyes misting with tears. They exit.

The Family Liaison Officer turns to DCI Fordham.

                    FAMILY LIAISON OFFICER
          I'm worried about her frame of
          mind. She described her brother's
          death as the best day of her life.
          I suspect there's a history of
          abuse.

                    DCI FORDHAM
          You think her brother's responsible?

                    FAMILY LIAISON OFFICER
              (nods)
          I think we barely scratched the
          surface.

                    DCI FORDHAM
          And you didn't keep her?

                    FAMILY LIAISON OFFICER
              (frustrated)
          On what basis? Her brother's dead.
          The immediate threat is gone.

                    DCI FORDHAM
          ...but the damage is already done.

The Family Liaison Officer nods, sad, exits.

Fordham looks down at the black business card Alicia gave
him. He frowns - puzzled: the name "Erin" is written in gold
lettering with a telephone number beneath.

INT. LAND ROVER - NIGHT

Alicia stares out the window at the passing street, lost in
her own world. Concerned, Jimmy The Fix puts his hand on her
shoulder. She shakes it off.

                    JIMMY THE FIX
          It's going to be okay. I have this
          under control.

                    ALICIA
          Is that what you told Lenny?

That floors Jimmy the Fix. A look of dark anger crosses his face.

                    JIMMY THE FIX
          Troy's going to pay. Believe me.

Alicia doesn't respond, keeps looking out the window.

INT. INTERROGATION ROOM, POLICE STATION - DAY

Troy sits at the table. A solemn looking DCI Fordham enters, drops a folder in front of Troy, who opens it.

                    TROY
          What's this?

                    DCI FORDHAM
          The ballistics report... The gun
          you used to kill Lenny Johnson is
          the same gun that killed...

                    TROY
              (Reading from the report)
          Quinlan Hearn...

A body blow for Troy.

DCI Fordham takes a seat opposite, pulls a mobile phone from an evidence bag.

                    DCI FORDHAM
          You recognise this?

Troy doesn't. DCI Fordham presses message replay.

                    TROY (O.S)
              (from the phone)
          ...If I have to come over there
          I'll kill you myself!

Troy closes his eyes, wrecked.

                    DCI FORDHAM
          I'm sorry, Troy. Jimmy's turned the
          tables on us. There's nothing I can
          do.

DCI Fordham holds the black business card between his fingers a beat, but whatever he was considering, he relents. He puts the card back into his pocket without Troy noticing it.

INT. CROWN COURT - DAY

Wood-veneered, old-school. Troy stands in the dock, glances to the public gallery. No sign of Tanya or his kids, but we do see a smiling Jimmy The Fix. Beside him Alicia looks stunning in her solemnity.

The JUDGE brings down his GAVEL:

> JUDGE
> ...Fifteen years for each of the three counts of murder, to run concurrently, with a minimum time served ten years.

Troy's head drops and he doesn't look up as the BAILIFF leads him out of the court room.

EXT. CROWN COURT - DAY

Jimmy The Fix exits alongside Alicia, he takes a deep breath, reaches for Alicia's arm but she pulls it away brusquely before turning her back.

DCI Fordham passes, noticing Jimmy too late, he steels himself.

> JIMMY THE FIX
> If there was any justice in this world, he'd be strung up for what he did.

They both watch Alicia striding away.

> DCI FORDHAM
> Do you ever wonder who her father is?

> JIMMY THE FIX
> What the fuck are you talking about?

> DCI FORDHAM
> Because there is no way that she's yours. I think there's some justice in that.

Jimmy's mouth twitches.

> JIMMY THE FIX
> Fuck you! Shut up or I'll...

> DCI FORDHAM
> (interrupting)
> Or you'll what? Punch me outside a court house? With all these witnesses?

                    JIMMY THE FIX
               You want witnesses? I can ruin you.
               Remember that.

Jimmy The Fix turns and follows Alicia.

INT. PRISON - DAY

Troy is led along a metal gantry by a GUARD.

In the background, the Gypsy Manfri watches as Troy is ushered into...

INT. PRISON CELL - DAY

Two bunks, a stainless steel toilet and nothing else.

INT. TROUBLE AND STRIFE PUB - DAY

An East End Pub scarred by years of grime and brawls. Now home to gutter THUGS and ALCOHOLICS.

TERRY "THE CANARY" FINCH, 56 - a greasy fry-up on legs - sits at the bar, a pint to his mouth...

But a hand takes the glass from Terry's lips and places it on the bar. Terry doesn't object as the hand belongs to...

Jimmy The Fix, who places himself next to Terry.

                    TERRY
               What's the word, Jimmy?

                    JIMMY THE FIX
               You're looking well Terry.

                    TERRY
               Thanks Jimmy. I like to keep in
               shape, you know? How're you? How's
               your Alicia?

                    JIMMY THE FIX
               None of your fucking business,
               Terry.

Jimmy peels two twenties onto the bar, gives a reassuring nod to Terry, who reaches for the money.

Jimmy slams the glass onto the back of Terry's hand.

                    JIMMY THE FIX (CONT'D)
               You know who I'm looking for?

Terry nods.

                    JIMMY THE FIX (CONT'D)
          I want them all. The wife and kids.
          But especially the boy.

                    TERRY
          Don't worry, I'll spread the word
          Jimmy.

INT. KITCHEN, SAFE HOUSE – DAY

Nothing more than a characterless box, cluttered with packing boxes through which a disheveled Tanya rifles.

A KNOCK at the door...

                    ERIN (O.S)
          I'll get it.

Erin appears, with DCI Fordham, who holds a bunch of flowers, awkward.

Tanya jumps up, embarrassed by her appearance.

                    TANYA
          Well. Here it is. We're still
          unpacking.

                    DCI FORDHAM
              (holding out flowers)
          I brought something to liven it up.

They both look awkwardly around.

                    TANYA
          Oh, maybe there's a vase...

Erin sits at the kitchen counter, writing out a postcard, a pleasant beach scene, absently stroking the tattoo on her neck. She glances at the exchange with a raised eyebrow.

DCI Fordham backs towards the doorway, Tanya follows.

                    DCI FORDHAM
          Well, it was just a quick hello. I
          didn't mean to... I'll call first.
          Next time.

                    TANYA
          Thank you. For everything.

She touches DCI's forearm. There's a sense of more to be said. DCI Fordham looks from Tanya to Erin, still watching, her head tilted, pulling several strands of hair into her mouth.

DCI FORDHAM
Well anyway. It was good to see you.

Tanya smiles at him as he squeezes through the smallest of gaps in the doorway.

ERIN
What the hell was that?

TANYA
Ancient history, that's all.

Erin understands.

ERIN
He's an ex, isn't he?

Tanya says nothing more, goes back to unpacking.

INT. PRISON CELL - DAY

Troy stares at his reflection in a makeshift mirror. The door opens behind him. Troy turns as Manfri enters the cell.

Troy recognises him immediately. Manfri pulls out a dangerous-looking shiv.

TROY
I didn't kill your brother.

MANFRI
The jury says otherwise.

Manfri attacks. He's skilled with the shiv. He slashes Troy across the chest, drawing blood. But Troy's fast too. He kicks Manfri away, smashing him against the wall. Manfri comes at Troy again. This time Troy grabs his arm, twists until Manfri drops the shiv.

Manfri swings with his left, clocks Troy, then unleashes a mad torrent of blows. Troy takes a few, before he rushes at Manfri, tackles him.

They roll on the floor, wrestling back and forth, until Troy manages to pin Manfri, pressing down on his throat.

TROY
I told you - I didn't kill your brother.

Troy releases Manfri, and jumps back.

TROY (CONT'D)
And I can prove to you who did.

INT. PRISON VISITING ROOM - DAY

Communal, a depressing row of formica tables and plastic chairs. Manfri sits across from Sandra...

>   SANDRA
> ...the Tasker brothers are siding with Chas now...

...but Manfri is really listening in on Troy's conversation with DCI Fordham at the adjoining table.

>   TROY
> You guaranteed their safety. From the outset, that was the whole point.
>
>   DCI FORDHAM
> I'm saying they're not in witness protection, but there are still measures I can take to keep them safe. Trust me...
>
>   TROY
> Trust you? What about me? I'm in here for a murder I didn't commit. I did not kill Quinlan Hearn.
>
>   DCI FORDHAM
> I know. If I could just get a warrant to get into Jimmy's safe, I'm sure we'd find evidence that puts the murder on him.
>
>   TROY
> So, what's the delay?
>
>   DCI FORDHAM
> I need probable cause to even get the warrant. And with your conviction, nobody else is interested in the case anymore...

Manfri looks from DCI Fordham to Troy. He's heard the whole thing.

>   SANDRA
> Are you listening to me?
>
>   MANFRI
> Yeah, yeah. The Tasker brothers. They're in here...

EXT. COMMERCIAL STRIP - DAY

Spider shows off a load of copper cabling in the back of a beat-up old pick-up truck to a BROKER at a scrap yard. The broker looks at the cabling, shakes his head.

Spider gets in the pick-up and drives off, down the decaying street, past a parade of fast food shops clinging to survival.

At the corner, he sees three YOUNG TOUGHS blocking the path of Cassie, the daughter of "King of the Gypsies" Chas McGregor.

> YOUNG TOUGH 1
> Girl like you, no business walking round here on her own. You get me?

Young Tough 1 grabs Cassie, as Young Tough 2 grabs her handbag. Cassie thrashes, tries to break free.

> YOUNG TOUGH 1 (CONT'D)
> Oh, you like to scrap, is it? Maybe we oughta teach you stinking little pikey a lesson, eh?

Young Tough 3 picks up her legs, and they manhandle her down the nearby alley.

Spider SCREECHES to a halt at the curb, piles out of his pick-up and quickly dispatches Young Tough 2 with his right fist, turns to...

Young Tough 3 who reaches into his clothes for a KNIFE. Spider catches him with a double chop to the throat and a kick to the groin.

Cassie BITES Young Tough 1's hand, stamps on his foot, breaking free as...

Spider HAMMERS his fist into Young Tough 1's face and kicks the prone Young Tough 2 in the groin a second time for good measure.

Spider grabs Cassie's purse and hustles her into his pick-up.

INT. RECREATION ROOM, PRISON - DAY

Troy watches television with the other INMATES.

Manfri mops the floor, oblivious to the approaching TASKER BROTHERS (30's) - two brutish inmates - making a bee-line towards him.

Tasker Brother 1 carries a SHIV discreetly in his hand, reaching Manfri he readies to thrust the shiv into Manfri's side...

                    TASKER BROTHER 1
               Message from Chas.

But Troy stamps on the back of Tasker Brother 1's ankle, grabbing his elbow as he staggers and, in one swift movement, swings his arm up, forcing the blade into his own shoulder.

Alerted, Manfri whacks the mop across the other brother's face, punches him twice in the throat.

Troy and Manfri exchange a glance and move away from the two fallen brothers, before the guards react.

INT. SPIDER'S PICK-UP, MOVING - DAY

Spider drives, Cassie at his side. Spider glances sideways at Cassie, who fiddles with her hair, looking directly at him with her big, deep eyes.

They arrive at the top of a lane.

                    CASSIE
               Here's fine.

Spider looks around: desolate, grim.

                    SPIDER
               I can take you closer. To wherever.

                    CASSIE
               Are you stupid or what? You get any
               closer and we both get slapped.
               Only you won't walk away.

                    SPIDER
               Why?

                    CASSIE
               We don't take well to gorgers.
                    (Off Spider's expression)
               Non-Gypsies.

                    SPIDER
               You're a Gypsy?

                    CASSIE
                 (snorts)
               My father calls himself "King of
               the Gypsies."

Spider digests that one, nods. He glances into the back of his truck.

                    SPIDER
               What if I've got reason not to get
               either of us slapped.

INT. RECREATION ROOM, PRISON - DAY

Manfri and Troy watch from a discreet distance as the GUARDS surround the two inmates.

                    TROY
          Friends of yours?

                    MANFRI
          Cousins.
              (Off Troy's expression)
          I know. Fucked up right? Suddenly
          I'm enemy number one because of
          some self appointed King of the
          Gypsies.

                    TROY
          You? Why?

                    MANFRI
              (mock seriousness)
          Because I am the one true King.

                    TROY
          You're serious?

                    MANFRI
              (nods)
          Chas is taking it very seriously.

EXT. SANDY BROOK TRAILER PARK - DAY

Spider drives through the gates past gleaming cars and caravans amidst a graveyard of rusting fairground rides, car entrails and a makeshift boxing ring.

Spider and Cassie exit the truck to hostile stares.

Chas leads the approach from his caravan as the rest of the CAMP draws around. Particularly interested is Casanova Kelly, who beat up Spider when they were teens. Casanova glares possessively at Cassie.

                    CHAS
          Who's this then?
              (to Spider)
          What are you doing with my
          daughter?

Spider looks to Cassie, she nods her encouragement and Spider reaches in to the rear of the pick-up. Cassie bats her eyelashes, playing cute for her father.

                    CASSIE
          He saved me from being mugged.

                    CASANOVA
          You shouldn't be walking around on
          your own out there.

Chas raises a hand to silence Casanova as Spider pulls back a
tarpaulin, reveals the copper cabling beneath.

                    SPIDER
          There's two grand's worth here,
          more even.

Chas LAUGHS.

                    CHAS
          Nah... Not worth the aggro.
              (meaning the sheathing)
          You still got the serial numbers
          for fuck's sake.

The rest of the group SNIGGER, especially Casanova.

                    SPIDER
          A grand.

                    CHAS
          Two hundred quid and that's a gift
          for bringing Cassie back safe.

Spider covers the cabling as the group turn their back.

                    SPIDER
          Forget it. I'll take it somewhere
          else.

                    CHAS
          Good luck with that.

Spider notices the punch bag and boxing ring, glances at
Cassie.

                    SPIDER
          I'll fight for it. Two grand, if I
          win. You keep the cabling if I lose.

The men stop walking away.

                    CASANOVA
          I'll take that fight.

EXT. SANDY BROOK BOXING RING - DAY

Casanova and Spider face off in the middle of the ring. Chas
steps in as referee, tucking the wager in his pocket.

The BELL RINGS. Spider lands a jab. Casanova shakes his head,
but comes back at Spider.

Spider steps back, brings his arms up defensively, and absorbs the blows.

Casanova gathers his breath. Spider's face is bloodied.

						SPIDER
				Come on. You punch like a girl.
				Hit me.

Spider laughs as Casanova connects with a series of heavy blows.

Then, as Casanova pauses, out of breath, Spider unleashes a counter jab, follows up with a wicked combination of belting punches. After this pounding, Casanova goes down, unmoving.

Spider smiles as he collects his money from Chas.

Spider spots Cassie striding away. Spider goes to follow, but Chas blocks his way.

						CHAS
				If I see you near my daughter
				again, I will kill you.
					(lets that sink in)
				But, if you want to stop wasting
				your time with that scrap and use
				these instead...
					(raises his fists)
				Then you let me know.

INT. PRISON CELL - DAY

Manfri shifts from foot to foot. His few personal belongings packed on the bed, he's ready to leave.

Troy sits on the edge of his bunk, gazes down at a divorce petition letter from Thysson Sherwood Solicitors.

						MANFRI
				You'll be alright?

						TROY
				Yeah. Don't worry about me.
					(meaning the letter)
				It was a long time coming.

A guard puts his head around the door, looks at Manfri.

						GUARD
				You ready to see the world again?

Manfri nods eagerly. Troy and Manfri embrace in a congratulatory hug.

						TROY
				Take care.

                    MANFRI
          I owe you. You ever need help, you
          come to me.

Troy nods his appreciation.

EXT. SANDY BROOK BOXING RING - DAY

A rough, fractious CROWD surrounds Spider, who dispenses a
LARGE BRUTE with a thunderous uppercut.

He plays to the crowd, some of whom use their cameras to
film.

As the crowd moves in to help the fallen fighter, Spider
pushes his way towards Chas, busy taking pay-outs, until he
bumps into Cassie.

They face each other awkwardly... Cassie slips Spider a note
in his hand. They look into each other's eyes...

Until, roughly, Casanova Kelly grabs her by the arm.

                    CASANOVA
              (hissing)
          You shouldn't be here.

                    CASSIE
              (resisting)
          Get off. You don't own me.

Casanova pushes her along.

                    SPIDER
          She said to leave her alone.

Casanova faces Spider as Cassie is caught in the flow of the
departing crowd.

                    CASANOVA
          You don't belong here, gorger.

Casanova steps back and is swallowed along in the crowd...

Spider unfolds the note, to reveal the words "BOAT HOUSE,
MIDNIGHT."

EXT. PRISON - DAY

The gates open, and a smiling Manfri exits, to find Sandra
waiting for him, caked in make-up, tottering in heels,
squeezed into a tight trashy dress, emphasising her ample
cleavage.

They embrace, she giggles then slaps him across the face.

                    SANDRA
          Next time you listen to me. I don't
          want you leaving me again. I have
          needs.

Sandra leans into him, starts groping Manfri. Manfri scans
the area warily.

                    MANFRI
          Leave it, love, not here. I don't
          want to be standing with my dick
          out if Chas turns up.

Manfri pushes a pouting Sandra towards the car.

EXT. BOAT HOUSE - NIGHT

Spider jogs along an overgrown path, overlooking a moonlit
lake. Up ahead is a FIGURE on a bench in front of a decaying
Boat House. Spider runs faster.

The figure stands... it is Cassie. She and Spider embrace,
hungrily kiss each other. Then, Spider picks her up, takes
her into the Boat House.

INT. VISITING ROOM, PRISON - DAY

Troy files in with the other prisoners, he spots Spider
sitting at a table, fiddling with the Four Leaf Glover around
his neck.

Troy slides into the seat opposite. They stare at each other,
eyes moist, battling back tears.

                    TROY
          What the hell are you doing here?

                    SPIDER
          I'm tired of living by other
          people's rules.

Troy scans the room, looks at the other faces.

                    TROY
          It's for your own safety. Jimmy's
          people could be watching me.

                    SPIDER
          I'm sorry we didn't come to the
          trial. Mom wouldn't let us. Erin
          was livid at her. Still is.

                    TROY
          I know. She wrote me.

Troy notices the FADING BRUISES on his son, frowns.

                TROY (CONT'D)
          Tell me you're not boxing again,
          too? You're supposed to be staying
          out of sight.

                POPOEYE
          Don't worry. I'm being careful.

                TROY
          You have to look after your sister
          and your mother.

                SPIDER
          There's something else. There's a
          girl.

Troy sees the excitement in Spider's eyes.

                TROY
          You in love with her?

                SPIDER
          Yeah. She's special.

Troy sits back, smiles.

                TROY
          Good for you, son. Nothing's better
          in life than first love. But all
          the more reason to be careful.
          Right?

Spider nods.

                TROY (CONT'D)
          So go on, get out of here before
          someone sees you.

                SPIDER
          Love you dad.

                TROY
          Love you.

Spider stands, exits. Troy watches him go.

INT. TROUBLE AND STRIFE PUB - DAY

Terry "The Canary" Finch sips a pint with Casanova Kelly.
They shake hands.

They both watch a video clip of Spider's boxing on Casanova's
phone.

EXT. SANDY BROOK BOXING RING - DAY

Spider dispatches another opponent in the makeshift ring. The CROWD CHEERS. But among them is Terry Finch, alongside Casanova Kelly. Terry smiles.

EXT. BOAT HOUSE - NIGHT

Spider runs through the park again, heading towards Cassie and the Boat House. She jumps up, a small bump evidence of her pregnancy. Cassie freezes...

THREE FIGURES emerge from behind the trees, between her and Spider. They swing lengths of pipe at Spider's head. Spider goes down, holding his neck.

Cassie stands, starts to run towards the fallen Spider, but he waves her away, even as the figures hit him over and over.

Cassie stops, watches for a moment in horror, then runs away, CRYING, into the darkness.

The figures finish off Spider. Then, one of them leans in and yanks Spider's FOUR LEAF GLOVER from his neck.

INT. VISITING ROOM, PRISON - DAY

Troy is seated, waiting, his face drops as...

Jimmy the Fix enters, makes a big show of looking around, plonks himself down.

> JIMMY THE FIX
> Backfired didn't it? Your clever little plan.

> TROY
> (rising to leave)
> I've got better things to do.

> JIMMY THE FIX
> I wanted to pass on my personal condolences...

Jimmy pulls his gold chain out of his shirt. On the end is Spider's FOUR LEAF GLOVER.

The colour drains from Troy's face.

> JIMMY THE FIX (CONT'D)
> It's a shame. He really was a pretty good fighter.

Now Jimmy stands as Troy GULPS for air.

                    JIMMY THE FIX (CONT'D)
               (hissing)
          I am nowhere near done. Believe me,
          I've barely even started.

Troy staggers, destroyed.

INT. SAFE HOUSE - DAY

Tanya puts up shelves with a nail gun. A KNOCK at the door.

Tanya opens it to reveal DCI Fordham, who looks at her grimly.

Tanya backs away from him, her hand flies to her mouth, her head shaking slowly, she breaks into tears. DCI Fordham moves to comfort her. She responds by hitting his shoulder over and over, finally running out of steam she leans in to him, sobbing.

Erin is drawn downstairs by the commotion. Reaching the bottom, her legs buckle at the sight of her mother sobbing on Fordham's shoulder. Erin hangs on to the bannister, then flies back up the stairs.

INT. VISITING ROOM, PRISON - DAY

Troy sits disconsolate, head in hands, staring at DCI Fordham opposite him.

                    TROY
          What about Tanya and Erin?

                    DCI FORDHAM
          I moved them again. Erin asked to
          be separated from her mother.

                    TROY
          She did?

                    DCI FORDHAM
          It is safer. But she's also angry
          at Tanya. Blames her for pushing
          Spider away.

                    TROY
          ...she should blame you.

                    DCI FORDHAM
          You want to apportion blame? Blame
          Spider. He's the one who wouldn't
          follow procedure. And you? You're
          in here for a reason. There's a
          limit to what I can do and I am
          trying my best...

                    TROY
          Jimmy came in here, flaunting the
          murder in my face...

                    DCI FORDHAM
          Really I am sorry, if there was
          anything...

                    TROY
          What about the funeral?

DCI Fordham considers a long beat.

                    DCI FORDHAM
          I can't let you go. But I'll
          arrange for you to visit the
          grave... it's less of a security
          risk.

Troy nods his agreement.

                    DCI FORDHAM (CONT'D)
          And there's this.

DCI Fordham slides across a black business card.

Troy turns it over in his hand: "Erin" written in gold lettering with her telephone number beneath.

INT. RECREATION ROOM, PRISON - DAY

Troy holds the business card, dials the number.

It goes straight to voicemail - a sexy, come-on voice:

                    VOICEMAIL (V.O.)
          This is Erin. You know what to do.

                    TROY
              (into the phone)
          Hi. It's Troy. I would like to talk
          to you. In person. I know who you
          really are.

INT. VISITING ROOM, PRISON - DAY

Alicia files in with the other visitors, drawing admiring glances. She sits in front of Troy.

EXT. SAFE HOUSE - DAY

DCI Fordham stands outside, he holds his hand out to Tanya as she exits. Dressed for a funeral.

INT. VISITING ROOM, PRISON - DAY

Alicia sits in front of Troy. He wipes away a tear:

          ALICIA
It started innocent enough. Almost like a normal brother. He'd lay next to me, just hanging out. Sometimes he would rock me... But his rocking turned to touching... Turned to groping... Until finally...

Beat.

          ALICIA (CONT'D)
At some point I realised I didn't feel angry anymore, I didn't hate, I didn't feel anything... The Alicia that you knew doesn't exist anymore, she died a long time ago.

          TROY
Did Jimmy know?

          ALICIA
If he did, he couldn't process it. When it came to Lenny he was blind to his faults...

Beat.

          TROY
There's something else... I think I'm...

          ALICIA
          (she cuts him off)
I know. Or I guessed. I keep thinking - what if I'd grown up in your house.

          TROY
I thought I was doing the right thing, leaving you with your mother.

          ALICIA
But she couldn't protect me.

          TROY
Sorry doesn't come close, I know that. But if you can find it in yourself to forgive me...

          ALICIA
You'll what? Welcome me with open arms...

Alicia sees her business card in Troy's hand.

                    ALICIA (CONT'D)
          A fucked up whore pretending to be
          the girl whose life I've always
          wanted. I'm sure Tanya would be
          delighted... Look, killing Lenny
          set me free and for that I'm
          grateful, but I don't need your
          salvation and I sure don't want
          your pity...

                    TROY
          It's not pity.

Troy studies Alicia a beat - finally...

                    TROY (CONT'D)
          Alicia, I have no right to ask
          this, but I need you to pass on a
          message for me...

INT. MANFRI'S TRAILER - NIGHT

Manfri escorts Sandra giggling towards the bedroom, but is
intercepted by...

Brendan and Billy Boswell who enter the caravan unannounced.
They head towards the laptop on the kitchen work top.

                    MANFRI
          Have you not heard of knocking?

                    BRENDAN
          You need to see this.

Brendan brings up a video clip on the laptop:

ANGLE ON LAPTOP SCREEN

Grainy, jerky video - it's a "CALL OUT".

Chas McGregor, flanked by Casanova and several pikeys, their
sleeves rolled up to their armpits, posture aggressively to
the camera.

                    CHAS MCGREGOR
          Ask anyone here and they'll tell you
          that I am the King of the Gypsies.
          You, Manfri? You're nothing but a
          mouthpiece, hiding in your wife's
          panties. You're a dirty, good for
          nothing coward. You think I'm not
          entitled to wear this?

Chas holds his King of the Gypsies medallion to the camera...

                    CHAS MCGREGOR (CONT'D)
          Then come and get it! I'm saying to
          you now. I'm ready to fight any
          time, any place, any where.

Manfri stops the video.

                    MANFRI
               (at the laptop)
          Any place, any where? It's the same
          fucking thing you moron.

Then, Manfri sees a dark shape move outside.

                    MANFRI (CONT'D)
          Sandra, get in the back.

                    SANDRA
          Not with that tone I won't.

                    MANFRI
          Can you just do as I say woman,
          without me having to explain
          myself?

Sandra sees Manfri is tense, and bites her tongue, heads towards the rear with a scowl.

                    MANFRI (CONT'D)
          Wait. Sandra come here.

Sandra turns.

                    SANDRA
          You're getting on my last nerve...

Manfri shuts her up with a big smothering kiss on the lips.

                    MANFRI
          Now get in the back. It could be
          Chas...

Manfri grabs a knife from the kitchen. He creeps outside.

EXT. MANFRI'S TRAILER - NIGHT

Rain is pouring. Brendan and Billy follow close behind Manfri. Nothing moves but the rain.

A THUNK comes from a decrepit looking trailer.

Approaching the trailer, Manfri reaches out slowly towards the door, he swings it open with a yell...

Cassie, bedraggled, cowers in a corner.

INT. MANFRI'S TRAILER - NIGHT

Cassie fights back tears, rubbing her hand over her swollen stomach.

CASSIE
I didn't know where else to go.

SANDRA
Don't you worry. What kind of father kicks out his own daughter?

Manfri's phone RINGS. He answers.

MANFRI
(into the phone)
Hello?

INT. ALICIA'S FLAT - NIGHT

ALICIA
(Into the phone)
I have a message from Troy...

INT. PRISON CELL - DAY

Troy puts the divorce petition letter and beach scene postcard from Erin into his pocket as the guard arrives.

EXT. CEMETERY - DAY

Grey, overcast, miserable. Troy stands shackled in front of a headstone in his own private ceremony, watched over by FOUR armed PRISONER ESCORTS.

In the distance a Land Rover stops.

INT. LAND ROVER - DAY

Manfri sits in the driver's seat next to Gypsy strong-man Brendan Boswell. In the back, fast-talking Billy Boswell, strains to see:

BILLY
Can we at least get a bit closer? We need to catch a bus from here.

BRENDAN
(doubtful)
It looks a bit boggy.

                        BILLY
            We're in a Land Rover, it's made
            for boggy, that's why it's called a
            fucking Land Rover.

Manfri exits the car, studying Troy and his escorts.

Brendan and Billy join him.

                        BILLY (CONT'D)
            I thought you said two?

Manfri nods.

                        BILLY (CONT'D)
            We need reinforcements.

                        MANFRI
                (To himself)
            Sorry Troy. I wish we could get
            Chas to help.

Deflated, Manfri turns back towards the car.

EXT. CEMETERY - DAY

Troy looks up and sees Manfri, Brendan and Billy in the distance, climbing back in to the Land Rover.

But suddenly, Troy is yanked sideways as his guards react to a disturbance...

SIX MEN IN BALACLAVAS

Overpower Troy's escorts with military finesse, throw a hood over Troy's head, and drag him into a van, then pile in after him.

INT. VAN, MOVING - DAY

One of the men pulls the hood from Troy's head.

Roman, Jimmy's right-hand man, smiles back at Troy from the driver's seat.

                        ROMAN
            Jimmy The Fix sends his regards.

But they are jolted forward as Roman slams on the brakes.

A Land Rover pulls across their path.

Then the side windows of the van SHATTER. Roman and the others flinch instinctively, look back up to...

EXT. ROAD - DAY

Manfri points a shotgun at their heads, leans in, removes the keys.

Billy yanks open the rear doors, shotgun trained inside, he beckons the shackled Troy out... as Brendan slashes the tyres.

Troy gets free of the van, runs to the Land Rover.

INT. DCI FORDHAM'S CAR - DAY

Fordham and Tanya arrive back at the safe house. Tanya hesitates before opening the passenger door, her eyes full of tears.

> TANYA
> Thank you.

She doesn't object when he takes her hand, lets it rest on her lap. She looks across at him and the tears flow. He puts his arm around her as she leans in to his shoulder.

> DCI FORDHAM
> If you could go anywhere... start over? Where would it be?

Tanya pulls back, looks at him.

> DCI FORDHAM (CONT'D)
> Do you remember when we first met? You would always say, what if...

> TANYA
> I was a teenager...

> DCI FORDHAM
> It's never too late...

DCI Fordham's mobile RINGS, he looks at the number, answers:

> DCI FORDHAM (CONT'D)
> Yes, what?
> (listens)
> He's what!?

DCI Fordham's face drops. Tanya senses something wrong, mouths her goodbyes and exits the car.

DCI Fordham watches her walk to the front door as he hangs up his phone, pulls away, and dials another number.

> JIMMY THE FIX (V.O)
> What?

DCI Fordham SHOUTS into the mobile:

                    DCI FORDHAM
          An armed assault? What the fuck
          were you thinking? This is way
          outside my control. You realise
          that? There is only so much
          interference I can run.

INT. REAR OFFICE, THE FIX - SIMULTANEOUS

Simmering, Jimmy stands in front of his desk with Roman,
YELLS into his phone:

                    JIMMY THE FIX
          Running interference? You are the
          fucking interference.

Jimmy ends the call.

INT. MANFRI'S TRAILER - NIGHT

Billy and Brendan cut off Troy's manacles with a bolt cutter.

Sandra cooks in the kitchen, trying to fend off Manfri who is
sampling the food, fondling her and searching drawers in
equal measure.

Manfri finds what he's looking for, and hands Troy a mobile
phone. Troy smiles his thanks.

                    TROY
          You want Jimmy dead, I get it, but
          this will hurt him more... And
          think what you can buy with it.

Sandra doles out four plates of bloated Spaghetti Bolognese.
Manfri adds a glob of mashed potato and a healthy squirt of
Ketchup and leaves them to it.

Manfri watches her move away.

                    MANFRI
               (quietly)
          A new trailer to start. She
          deserves something nice.

                    BILLY
          I guess there's no harm in taking a
          look...

Brendan nods his agreement reluctantly.

INT. THE FIX - NIGHT

Terry "The Canary" Finch devours a plate of pie and mash,
gravy dripping from his chin.

Jimmy the Fix sits alongside. Roman stands over them. They are given wide berth by the girls and punters.

          TERRY
I tell you he's gone to ground Jimmy. There's been no word on the street since he escaped.

Jimmy shoves Terry's face cheek down into his food, comes in close...

          JIMMY THE FIX
That's because he's not on the street. I want to sit down with the pikey you used to sort out Troy's kid.

          TERRY
Him? Not easy, he moves around a lot.

Jimmy presses Terry's head harder in to the plate.

          JIMMY THE FIX
Can you do it?

Terry nods the best that he can and Jimmy releases his grip.

          JIMMY THE FIX (CONT'D)
You understand that time is of the essence Terry.

Terry rights himself, wiping the food from his face.

          TERRY
Yes Jimmy.

          JIMMY THE FIX
Fuck off then.

Jimmy shoves him away with his foot.

INT. LAND ROVER - NIGHT

Troy, Manfri, Billy and Brendan are parked across the street from:

EXT. THE FIX - NIGHT

A few PATRONS enter past the doorman as Terry "the Canary" Finch exits, still wiping his face. He waddles down the street, oblivious as:

INT. LAND ROVER - NIGHT

Troy ducks out of view.

Once Terry has gone, Manfri motions to Troy, and they exit the Land Rover, pulling on high-vis jackets. They head towards a TURKISH CONVENIENCE STORE in the neighbouring building.

Two GIRLS, about 20 - curvaceous, flirtatious - walk by the Land Rover, approaching the Fix, their bums swaying.

Billy appreciates the view:

                BILLY
      Cushty sorts.

Billy reaches across Brenden, presses the car HORN. Brenden brushes Billy's hands away.

              FAT GEORGE
      Don't reach across the driver.

The girls smile coyly...

                BILLY
      You're not fucking driving.

              FAT GEORGE
      (gesturing around him)
      This is still the driving zone.

INT. TURKISH CONVENIENCE STORE - NIGHT

Manfri and Troy accompany the SHOP OWNER, 60 - smiley - to the rear of the store and into...

INT. STORE ROOM, TURKISH CONVENIENCE STORE - NIGHT

To a frosted window, sealed shut under layers of paint. Distant POUNDING of music from The Fix. Troy sticks his eye close to a scratch in the frosting.

TROY'S POV

Through the scratch he sees a slither of a lightwell and to the side, another frosted window protected by a wire mesh.

Troy nods to Manfri, who hands the Shop Owner some bills.

INT. THE FIX - NIGHT

Billy and Brendan approach the bar, order beers and survey the place.

No sign of Jimmy the Fix, but there is an overt security presence, with BOUNCERS placed strategically throughout the club.

The TWO GIRLS from outside emerge from the rear, in flimsy underwear. They glide provocatively towards the two boys.

                    BILLY
          Quick, photograph.

Before they can object Billy hangs on to the two girls, his arms around their shoulders.

Brendan takes a few quick photographs of Billy and the Girls, surreptitiously capturing the club in the background.

Billy returns the favour, taking pictures of Brendan with different angles of the club.

Two bouncers move in.

                    BOUNCER 1
          No photographs.

Billy and Brendan are herded towards the exit.

INT. SAFE HOUSE - NIGHT

Fordham paces, agitated, in front of a puzzled Tanya.

                    DCI FORDHAM
          We could leave tomorrow. Start
          over. Anywhere you want.

                    TANYA
          (laughing)
          Be serious. You're going to give up
          the Force, everything you've worked
          for? Just like that?

                    DCI FORDHAM
          To hell with the Force. I've given
          everything and it just keeps on
          taking. Loyalty is a one way
          street.

Beat.

                    TANYA
          I appreciate everything that you've
          done for us. For me. If it wasn't
          for you... God knows what else
          would have happened...

                    DCI FORDHAM
          But?

                    TANYA
          I can't trust my own feelings right
          now? You understand? I need time,
          can you give me that?

                    FORDHAM
          I'll try.

He nods, but it's unconvincing.

EXT. STREETS - NIGHT

Troy, Manfri, Billy and Brendan drive through the quiet,
seedy streets.

                    BILLY
          More security than we could handle.

Troy nods in agreement, as he pulls the divorce petition
letter from his pocket and looks at the return address:
Thysson Sherwood Solicitors.

INT. LAND ROVER - NIGHT

They park and all look across at...

EXT. HIGH STREET OFFICE BUILDING - NIGHT

A nondescript four-story professional office.

INT. CORRIDOR, THYSSON SHERWOOD SOLICITORS - NIGHT

Dark after hours. Troy arrives at a nameplate announcing
"Thysson Sherwood Solicitors."

Troy quickly picks the lock and enters:

INT. OFFICE, THYSSON SHERWOOD SOLICITORS - NIGHT

Messy. Files piled haphazardly.

Troy taps a keyboard, a screen lights up - but it's password
protected, he searches through the desk clutter.

Billy and Brendan walk past the office lugging computer
equipment.

A commotion outside the office and Manfri appears, shoves a
SOLICITOR (late 40's) - prissy - into the office.

                    BILLY
          Found him coming out the shitter.
          Says we need an appointment.

                    TROY
               (points to the PC)
          What we need is access to this.

                    SOLICITOR
          That's not mine... and it's
          confidential.

Manfri clips the back of his head.

                    TROY
          You got family...?

                    SOLICITOR
          Yes.

                    TROY
          Me too. Do anything to keep them
          safe right?

The solicitor nods.

                    TROY (CONT'D)
          So, if I tell you my family is in
          immediate danger, you'll understand
          that I will do anything to help
          them?

Nervous nodding.

                    TROY (CONT'D)
          Even if that means hurting you?

Troy pulls the chair out.

                    TROY (CONT'D)
          So if I give you the opportunity to
          save my family, then you'd take
          it...

The Solicitor takes the chair, refers to the letter, makes a
few key strokes and leans towards the screen.

                    SOLICITOR
               (pointing)
          There!

Troy scribbles on a post-it.

INT. BEDROOM, SAFE HOUSE - NIGHT

Faint streetlight seeps through a crack in the curtain. Tanya
lies in bed, stares up at the ceiling, restless.

A gloved hand smothers her face. Duct tape covers her mouth.
A cloth bag goes over her head.

INT. MANFRI'S TRAILER - NIGHT

Tanya is led into the trailer, and the bag is pulled off to reveal...

Troy, looking at his wife warily.

Tanya rips off the duct tape.

              TANYA
        (furious)
    Have you lost your bloody mind?

She spins around, searching for an escape, but Troy stands between her and the door.

Tanya bangs on the window. Troy tries to stop her. She thrashes her arms violently.

              TANYA (CONT'D)
    You get off me! Now!

Troy backs off, hands in the air.

              TROY
    Please? Just hear me out.

Tanya still looks like she wants to kill him.

              TROY (CONT'D)
    I know how it looks.

              TANYA
    Kidnapping! That's how it looks.

              TROY
    You have every right to be angry.

              TANYA
    Angry doesn't even begin... What are you even doing out?

              TROY
    Trying to protect you.

              TANYA
    Because you've done such a great fucking job so far?

Beat.

              TROY
    You're right...

              TANYA
    ...Good then!

                    TROY
          I can't change what's done, but
          I'll be damned if Jimmy gets away
          with it.

                    TANYA
          You're talking about revenge?

                    TROY
          Yeah.

                    TANYA
          It doesn't bring him back. It
          doesn't bring Spider back.

                    TROY
          It doesn't. But Jimmy's not done...

Beat. Tanya looks into Troy's eyes with fire:

                    TANYA
          Promise me one thing: you find
          Jimmy, you rip his fucking heart
          out!

EXT. SAFE HOUSE - NIGHT

DCI Fordham arrives at Tanya's safe house. He enters.

INT. BEDROOM, SAFE HOUSE - NIGHT

From the other room, we hear Fordham yelling:

                    DCI FORDHAM (O.S.)
          Tanya? Where are you?

Fordham runs into the run, worried.

                    DCI FORDHAM (CONT'D)
          Tanya?

He sees signs of the struggle around her bed - lamp and table knocked over. His colour drains, and he slumps on the bed.

INT. MANFRI'S TRAILER - DAY

Troy sits at the laptop with various photographs of the Turkish Convenience Store and the Fix open on the screen.

Sandra sits on Manfri's lap - they canoodle like teenagers. Billy and Brendan listen carefully as Troy finishes running through the plan.

Tanya is in the background, looking at Troy with concern.

                    TROY
          Jimmy's security will be halved
          when he leaves

                    BILLY
          So we case the club?

Troy nods.

                    BRENDAN
          At least the scenery's fantastic.
          Those dancers...

Brendan kisses his fingers like they are a tasty dish.

                    TROY
          Everybody ready?

They all stand as Troy hefts the tool bag on to his shoulder.
They look to each other.

                    MANFRI
          For Quinlan.

                    BILLY
          Fuck yeah.

Manfri hugs and kisses Sandra goodbye, gropes her bum.

                    MANFRI
          Goodbye my love. We'll have some of
          the good stuff when I get back.

Manfri, Billy and Brendan pile out of the caravan. Troy pulls
Tanya aside, gives her the divorce petition back.

                    TROY
          I know I've fallen short, as a
          husband and a father, but I never
          stopped loving you... I want you to
          be happy. With or without me. You
          deserve it...

                    TANYA
          I don't know what I want right now.

Troy pulls out Alicia's black business card.

                    TROY
          If anything happens to me... can
          you call this number.

                    TANYA
          Our Erin?

Troy shakes his head.

                         TROY
               It's actually Alicia. I abandoned
               her once. I promised myself I won't
               do it again.

Tanya's heckles rise.

                         TANYA
               How is this my responsibility?

                         TROY
               It's mine, but she needs someone
               kind and strong to help her. Like
               you.

Tanya softens, nods and slots the card in the breast pocket of her blouse.

INT. REAR OFFICE, THE FIX - DAY

Jimmy the Fix paces, looking impatiently at his phone. There's a KNOCK at the door.

                         ROMAN (O.S.)
               Someone to see you Jimmy.

                         JIMMY THE FIX
               Tell them to fuck off.

                         DCI FORDHAM (O.S)
               You're out of control, Jimmy.

Jimmy turns towards DCI Fordham and Roman at the door. Jimmy's mouth twitches.

                         DCI FORDHAM (CONT'D)
               Leave Troy's family out of this.

                         JIMMY THE FIX
                    (breathing deeply)
               You're getting cold feet now? It's
               too late for that, Fordham.

                         DCI FORDHAM
               No it's not.

                         JIMMY THE FIX
                    (pointing to the club)
               Half the girls out there know you.
               And now you're implicated in Troy's
               escape. You want to throw your
               whole life away?
                    (motions)
               Now sit. And listen to me. Here's
               what you're going to do for me.

DCI Fordham nods, but instead of sitting, he reaches inside his jacket. In a fast, smooth motion, he pulls out a gun and FIRES point-blank at Jimmy, who's flung against his safe.

Roman reacts quickly, delivering a fast chop to Fordham's neck. Fordham goes down in a heap, and the gun CLATTERS free.

Roman picks it up, turns to Jimmy, who GROANS in the corner. Then, Jimmy's GROANS turn to LAUGHTER.

Roman helps Jimmy to his feet. Jimmy feels the middle of his chest. Pulls out Spider's Four Leaf Glover medallion, now dented. Jimmy is giddy from the near-death experience.

> JIMMY THE FIX (CONT'D)
> The devil is on my side.

Jimmy goes to his desk, opens a drawer, pulls out a nail gun, nods to Roman, who drags the GASPING Fordham to the chair. Roman pulls out one of Fordham's hands, slaps it down on the desk.

Jimmy FIRES a nail into the back of Fordham's hand. Fordham SCREAMS.

Then they repeat with his other hand. Fordham passes out.

> JIMMY THE FIX (CONT'D)
> (to Fordham)
> Don't you go anywhere.

Roman follows Jimmy from the room.

EXT. THE FIX - DAY

Billy and Brendan, in high-vis jackets and hard hats, erect protective barriers in front of The Fix. They watch as Jimmy, Roman, and a few bodyguards file out of the club.

Billy sends a text message: "now."

EXT. TURKISH CONVENIENCE STORE - DAY

Manfri gets the text. He and Troy exit the Land Rover, also in high-vis jackets and hard hats. They collect tools and a step ladder and head into...

INT. TURKISH CONVENIENCE STORE - DAY

Troy and Manfri are greeted like family by the Shop Owner, who leads them to...

INT. STORE ROOM, TURKISH CONVENIENCE STORE - DAY

Troy moves towards the frosted window, pulling hammer and chisel from his tool bag.

INT. BOXING GYM - DAY

Spit and sawdust - a hostile mix of steroids and attitude. Young men pumping iron, sparring in a practice ring.

Casanova works out, hitting a punching bag. The bag is caught - Terry "The Canary" Finch smiles obsequiously at Casanova. Behind him are Jimmy The Fix and Roman.

Jimmy waves Terry away.

>   JIMMY THE FIX
>   You can go.

>   TERRY
>   But...

Roman pulls Terry away. Jimmy talks quietly, seriously to Casanova:

>   JIMMY THE FIX
>   I appreciate your help with Spider
>   Glover.

Casanova nods, warily. Jimmy hands him a thick envelope of cash.

>   JIMMY THE FIX (CONT'D)
>   If I was to say his old man had
>   joined up with a bunch of your
>   kind, no offence, would you have
>   any idea where that might be?

>   CASANOVA KELLY
>   I just might.

INT. STORE ROOM, TURKISH CONVENIENCE STORE - DAY

Troy heaves on the frosted window and it slides upwards reluctantly. He manoeuvres himself into the lightwell.

Manfri feeds the ladder through and then clambers after Troy, carrying duffel bags.

EXT. LIGHTWELL - DAY

Narrow, forgotten. Troy examines the security mesh in front of The Fix's frosted window, extracts an angle-grinder from his tool bag and... waits. Manfri taps a text into his phone: "drill."

In the background a PNEUMATIC DRILL starts and Troy smiles, applies the angle-grinder to the mesh...

EXT. THE FIX - DAY

Billy and Brendan DRILL the sidewalk.

INT. THE FIX - DAY

At the door to the back hallway, the bouncer hears the sound of the PNEUMATIC DRILL over the club MUSIC. He watches the girls and customers.

EXT. LIGHTWELL - DAY

Troy finishes cutting through the wire mesh. He pulls it off, and climbs through the frosted glass.

EXT. THE FIX - DAY

Billy and Brendan still drill, but at the sight of a POLICE OFFICER walking towards them, they throw their tools into the truck and walk on.

INT. REAR CORRIDOR, THE FIX - DAY

Troy and Manfri quietly make their way across the hallway, to Jimmy The Fix's office door. Troy kneels, picks the lock.

INT. THE FIX - DAY

Billy and Brendan Boswell enter, stuffing their high-vis jackets and hard hats out of sight.

They join the early punters, mingling with the dancers.

INT. REAR OFFICE, THE FIX - DAY

Troy and Manfri enter to find DCI Fordham slumped at Jimmy's desk, unconscious.

                    MANFRI
          Fuck me. Your gavver friend.

Troy goes directly to him, feels for a pulse.

                    TROY
          He's still alive.

                    MANFRI
          A bit attached to his desk isn't
          he?

Troy heads to the safe, runs his hand over the front.

                    TROY
               (to Manfri)
          Why aren't they drilling?

Manfri pulls out his mobile and dials.

INT. THE FIX - DAY

Billy has his mobile to his ear. Brendan grows increasingly rowdy.

                    BILLY
               (into the mobile)
          Gavvers are outside... but crack
          on. We've switched to plan B.

Brendan starts grinding behind a DANCER, drawing the bouncer's attention. Billy jumps up on the bar, and starts dancing.

                    BILLY (CONT'D)
          I'm on top of the world!

The bouncer comes running.

                    BOUNCER
          Hey! Get down!

INT. REAR OFFICE, THE FIX - DAY

The YELLING is audible in the background. Troy goes at the safe with the drill. The lock falls to the floor. Troy swings the safe open.

INSIDE: bundled cash, envelopes, drugs, guns and six large red ledgers.

Manfri scoops the money into their duffel bags as Troy flicks through the ledgers, astounded.

INT. THE FIX - DAY

The bouncer throws both Brendan and Billy out the front door.

They wink at each other and rush back inside taking the bouncers scrum-like to the ground.

EXT. TURKISH CONVENIENCE STORE - DAY

Troy and Manfri exit carrying three duffel bags between them.

INT. TURKISH CONVENIENCE STORE - DAY

DCI Fordham is laid out on his back in the store room, watched over by the Shop Owner, who is on the phone:

>   SHOP OWNER
>   (into phone)
>   I have a medical emergency...

EXT. TURKISH CONVENIENCE STORE - DAY

Troy and Manfri get into the Land Rover, duffel bags in hand. Billy and Brendan are waiting for them.

>   BILLY
>   Cushty.

>   TROY
>   Nice work, boys.

Brendan starts up the Land Rover, drives them off.

INT. MANFRI'S TRAILER - DAY

Tanya uses her tools to re-attach a kitchen cupboard securely: she stashes a screwdriver in her back pocket as she drills a new hole. Sandra helps out.

Cassie retches in the background, comes back wiping her mouth.

>   TANYA
>   How far gone are you?

>   CASSIE
>   4 Months.

>   TANYA
>   Where's the father?

Cassie battles to keep the tears in check.

>   TANYA (CONT'D)
>   Sorry, none of my business. In my
>   experience you're better off
>   without him.

>   CASSIE
>   He's dead.

                    TANYA
          Oh Cassie... What about your
          parents?

                    CASSIE
          They don't want me. Bad enough I'm
          not married, but I'm pregnant to a
          gorger.

Tanya can only shake her head.

                    CASSIE (CONT'D)
          It's okay. Manfri and Sandra have
          made me welcome.

                    SANDRA
              (smiling)
          You know that was just to stick it
          to your father.

A wan smile from Cassie.

                    TANYA
          What about names?

                    CASSIE
          Little Ben. After his father.

                    TANYA
          Ben?

                    CASSIE
          Yeah Ben, but everybody called
          him...

          CASSIE (CONT'D)   TRISHA
Spider.   Spider?

EXT. MANFRI'S TRAILER - DAY

TWO LAND ROVERS skid to a halt, the car doors are thrown open
as...

Sandra exits the disused trailer to meet them.

JIMMY THE FIX and his bodyguards exit the cars, along with
CASANOVA. All bear down on Sandra.

Roman pulls out a gun and FIRES POINT BLANK... Sandra is
THROWN backwards like a rag doll. DEAD before she hits the
ground.

INT. LAND ROVER, MOVING - DAY

Brendan, Billy, Troy and Manfri are pumped after their
successful heist.

INT. REAR OFFICE, THE FIX - DAY

Jimmy walks into his office, stops when he sees the wide-open, empty safe.

EXT. MANFRI'S TRAILER - DAY

The Land Rover pulls up. Manfri is the first to burst from the car. He runs to the dead body of Sandra, and cradles her in his arms, SCREAMING IN ANGUISH.

In a panic, Troy runs into the trailer:

INT. MANFRI'S TRAILER - DAY

Empty, but signs of a struggle. The new shelves are knocked off the wall, goods scattered about.

Troy, shell-shocked, fumbles as he gets out his RINGING mobile.

INT. REAR OFFICE, THE FIX - DAY

Jimmy the Fix stares at the empty safe.

          JIMMY THE FIX
    (into phone)
 Troy, You are a dead man. If you're not back here in an hour I will gut the pikey bitch sitting in front of me and I'll rip your grandson from her belly.

          TANYA (O.S.)
    (shouts)
 Troy!

Jimmy turns from the safe to Tanya and Cassie seated in front of Jimmy's bodyguards.

Roman SLAPS Tanya hard across her face.

EXT. MANFRI'S TRAILER - DAY

Troy watches Manfri in the background, rocking back and forth, cradling Sandra's dead body.

          TROY
    (in to mobile)
 You can have it all. If they remain unharmed. Touch either of them and you get nothing. I'll call you back.

Troy ends the call.

INT. REAR OFFICE, THE FIX - DAY

Jimmy the fix looks at his phone apoplectic. Looks like he wants to throw it. Instead, he grabs Tanya by the back of her neck, brings her face to his.

				JIMMY THE FIX
			Fucker hung up on me.

Tanya pulls her face away, but her proximity to Jimmy has a calming effect.

				JIMMY THE FIX (CONT'D)
			I always liked you... You were a
			stuck up bitch, but there was
			something.

ANGLE ON Jimmy's hand as it wanders down Tanya's lower back, over her left buttock, just misses the screwdriver in her rear right pocket. Jimmy's hand moves upwards, he grabs her breast predatorily. Tanya squirms, revulsed.

Jimmy's hand lands on the business card in her breast pocket, he pulls it out and looks at it, sees Erin's name and the number, then pushes Tanya away, smiling.

Jimmy hands the card to Roman, WHISPERS to him. Roman leaves.

EXT. MANFRI'S TRAILER - DAY

Manfri bears down on Troy, snatches the phone, puts it to his ear, it's dead.

				MANFRI
			Is that him?

				TROY
			He wants to deal... What does he
			mean grandson?

Manfri pushes Troy out of the way, heads towards his truck. Troy stops him from getting into the truck.

				TROY (CONT'D)
			Wait.

Manfri hauls him out of the way and throws him against the trailer.

				MANFRI
			Deal what? He's killed my wife and
			my brother. There ain't no deal.

				TROY
			It's suicide.

Manfri yanks Troy's collar tight. Billy and Brendan jump in to help Troy.

> MANFRI
> I don't owe you anything anymore. I should've let them string you up in the first place. I am this close to killing you right now.

Troy struggles against Manfri.

> TROY
> I want him as much as you do. But we can't do it alone. We need help.

INT. CORRIDOR, FAIRMOUNT HOTEL – DAY

Alicia knocks on a hotel room door. It opens, and she enters.

EXT. FAIRMOUNT HOTEL – DAY

Alicia steps in, unbuttoning her blouse, but is met with Roman, holding a gun.

EXT. SANDY BROOK TRAILER PARK – DAY

Troy and Manfri exit the car and are immediately surrounded by menacing GYPSIES.

No way out. One of the gypsies shoves Troy, who shoves back and the Gypsies move in on Troy and Manfri as...

Chas appears at the door to his trailer, King of the Gypsies.

INT. CHAS MCGREGOR'S TRAILER – DAY

Troy and Manfri sit with Chas.

> CHAS
> What's in it for me?

> TROY
> What about saving your own daughter?

> CHAS
> You're a gorger – you don't know anything. She's disgraced the McGregor name.

> MANFRI
> What about your grandson?

Chas glances at Troy, looks to be softening.

                         CHAS
               No.

                         MANFRI
               He's killed Quinlan and Sandra.
               Your own kind. You want to be King
               of the Gypsies? Then stand up and
               be King of all gypsies, not just
               King of some.

Chas is unmoved.

                         MANFRI (CONT'D)
               Forget it, we're wasting time with
               this coward.

They stand and exit.

EXT. SANDY BROOK TRAILER PARK - DAY

Troy and Manfri head back to the truck, watched on by Chas
McGregor and the rest of the Gypsies.

                         CHAS
               If anybody's a coward it's you.

MURMURS of agreement. Manfri turns to face Chas McGregor.

                         MANFRI
               Fine. You want that fight? Come and
               get it.

Troy puts a restraining hand out to Manfri.

                         TROY
                    (to Manfri)
               Wait.
                    (to Chas)
               I'll fight you.

                         CHAS
               I ain't fighting no gorger. You've
               no right to be King of the Gypsies.

                         TROY
               I'm not interested in your title.
               If I win, we leave together,
               everybody here, and we save your
               daughter. And our grandson. If I
               lose... Well then that's your
               choice...

EXT. SANDY BROOK BOXING RING - DAY

Chas McGregor, fists raised, sizes up Troy, throws an exploratory punch. Troy counters with a combination of punches.

Chas leans into the crowd, and they propel him back towards Troy. Chas wraps his arms around Troy's neck. Troy throws a series of punches to his kidneys.

Chas pushes Troy back into the crowd, and they grab Troy's arms, leave him defenceless as Chas hammers home a series of punches to Troy's ribs, jabs to the face.

Manfri tries to intervene but is restrained by the crowd.

Troy drops to his knee, blood pours from his lip and brow.

Emboldened, Chas beckons Troy forward.

Troy hauls himself up, advances. Chas ducks and counters in a slapping motion. Troy parries and attacks again, catches Chas with punch after punch.

Chas goes down on hands and knees at the crowd's feet.

An iron bar is dropped by Chas' hand, he curls his fingers around the shaft and swings the bar upwards and outwards - CRACK against Troy's head.

Chas swings again - CRUNCH against Troy's arm, Troy slips.

Chas stamps on Troy's outstretched ankle, moves in quickly, raising the bar above his head, he swings down.

Troy rolls and springs with his good leg, catches the bar with his good arm, yanking it from Chas' fingers, head butts Chas.

Chas staggers back, blood streaming from his nose, charges Troy with a snarl.

Troy swings his good arm with all his remaining strength, smashes Chas full in the face.

Chas is propelled backwards, lands on his back, finished, his "King of the Gypsies" pendant rests between his split and bloodied lips.

EXT. SANDY BROOK TRAILER PARK - DAY

Troy, bloodied, stands in front of Chas and the others, all armed.

                    TROY
               (into mobile)
          I'll meet you at a neutral venue.
          Not there...

INT. REAR OFFICE, THE FIX - DAY

Jimmy smiles, on his mobile:

                    JIMMY THE FIX
          We meet at the old boat house in an
          hour. The same place your son died.

Jimmy hangs up, gestures to the bodyguard that Tanya and
Cassie are to accompany them. The bodyguard applies two
hoods.

                    JIMMY THE FIX (CONT'D)
          Gather up the troops. All of them.

Roman hands the black business card back to Jimmy.

                    ROMAN
          What about the tart?

                    JIMMY THE FIX
          Have her brought to the lake too. I
          made Troy a promise I intend to
          keep.

EXT. BOAT HOUSE - NIGHT

Troy stands alone.

Headlights race down the drive towards him, and 4 Land Rovers
pull up in front of him.

Jimmy exits the lead vehicle, as a security detail of a DOZEN
MEN exit the other Land Rovers. Roman drags Tanya and Cassie,
hooded and bound, from the rear two vehicles.

Casanova is still with them.

Jimmy looks to Troy with contempt.

                    JIMMY THE FIX
          Where is it?

Walking with a pronounced limp, Troy leads Jimmy to the Boat
House. Roman follows, holding Tanya and Cassie tightly.

ANGLE ON Manfri, watching, hidden by the dense growth. He
flashes a torch, signalling into the darkness.

Casanova stands amongst the henchmen who take position by the
cars, shotguns at the ready.

INT. BOAT HOUSE - NIGHT

A large dusty room, with a few broken pieces of furniture. The door opens and Jimmy the Fix gives Troy a helping shove inside. Roman marches Tanya and Cassie into a corner. Jimmy pulls out a torch, sweeps the empty room.

The duffel bags are there, but the journals are missing.

>   JIMMY THE FIX
>   Where's the rest of it?

Troy turns, his face bruised, cuts to his lips and brow.

>   TROY
>   Once I know that they're safe. Then
>   you get the rest.

Jimmy doubles Troy over with a pile-driving blow to the ribs. Troy retches, scrabbling one-handed for a hold against the wall, protecting his other arm, but loses his footing.

>   JIMMY THE FIX
>   They'll never be safe Troy. You've
>   seen to that already.

ANGLE ON Tanya's hands, her fingers stretching into her rear right pocket. She angles it from the pocket and starts to attack the masking tape around her wrists.

EXT. BOAT HOUSE - NIGHT

A van speeds up the drive, and SCREECHES to a halt.

Two more HENCHMEN exit, dragging a hooded and bound Alicia with them towards the Boat House.

INT. BOAT HOUSE - NIGHT

Troy hauls himself to his feet, but is too slow - Jimmy grabs him, hurls him across the room.

>   TROY
>   This is between you and me. They
>   don't need to be part of it.

Jimmy replies with a fist to Troy's face.

The door opens, and the henchmen throw the bound gagged and hooded Alicia inside, next to Cassie and Tanya. Roman covers them all.

Troy, bleeding profusely, his face pounded and swollen, climbs up the wall, gasping for air, holding his side, and peers out the window:

EXT. BOAT HOUSE - NIGHT

He sees movement outside the trailer. Billy and Brendan slink up to Manfri, who signals into the darkness one more time.

Figures seem to materialise from the darkness, swarming Jimmy's security detail. A few SHOTS are FIRED, but the surprise is so sudden, that the henchmen's shotguns are useless and the fight quickly becomes a close quarters hail of fists.

We see Chas leading the fight, along with his band of Gypsies. Billy, Brendan and Manfri join the fray.

INT. BOAT HOUSE - NIGHT

Jimmy hears the GUNSHOTS, is momentarily distracted. He pulls his own gun, signals to Roman:

> JIMMY THE FIX
> Check it out.

Roman exits. Tanya uses the diversion to rush at Jimmy with the screwdriver. Jimmy blocks, pistol-whips her across the face and the screwdriver CLATTERS to the floor.

Jimmy drags a resistant Cassie towards the table, bends her over, her face hitting the table with a THUD. Troy tries to stand, but it's a struggle:

> TROY
> Don't do this.

Jimmy looks out the window, sees only darkness. He presses Cassie's face down on the table as he waves his gun at Troy.

> JIMMY THE FIX
> I swore to you.

Jimmy rips at Cassie's clothing. Cassie SCREAMS.

EXT. BOAT HOUSE - NIGHT

The battle rages. Gypsies and Jimmy's men trade blows.

Billy is about to be butted by a henchman's shotgun, but Brendan swings a fist into the man's face, staggering him. Billy grabs the gun away, swings it, knocking the wind out of the man. Brendan and Billy hold him upright as Manfri approaches, grabs hold of the man's throat:

> MANFRI
> You want to get out of here alive,
> you tell me who shot my wife...

The henchman gestures weakly towards Roman, who fights two other Gypsies at the door to the Boat House.

Manfri lets the henchman's head drop and Brendan and Billy carry him off into the darkness.

Manfri battles his way through the remaining fighters, reaches the door where Roman punches out one of the Gypsies. Then Roman turns to face Manfri. Other Gypsies move in too.

                    MANFRI (CONT'D)
          He's mine.

INT. BOAT HOUSE - NIGHT

Jimmy unbuckles a SCREAMING, fighting Cassie's jeans.

In a desperate final burst of strength, Troy charges Jimmy, knocks him clear of Cassie.

EXT. BOAT HOUSE - NIGHT

Chas KO's a henchman, comes face to face with Casanova.

                    CHAS
          How much that gorger Jimmy paying
          you?

                    CASANOVA
          None of your business, old man.

                    CHAS
          You know the punishment for
          disobeying the King.

                    CASANOVA
          You won't be King for long. I'm
          going to take that title now.

Chas smiles, raises his fists:

                    CHAS
          Bring it, dog.

Casanova squares off, and launches a rapid, brutal series of punches. Chas fends them off, returns fire.

INT. BOAT HOUSE - NIGHT

Troy and Jimmy crash to the ground, brawling.

Jimmy is the first to recover, swings his gun to cover Troy and grabs for the nearest hostage.

                             JIMMY
                   You win.

He pulls off the hood, to reveal Alicia, disheveled and
gagged, eyes adjusting, silently pleading with Jimmy. It is
difficult to distinguish her from Erin, save for the absence
of the tattoo on her neck.

Before anybody else can react, Jimmy brings the gun to her
head... and SHOOTS, snuffing out her life in an instant.

Troy scrambles to her body as Jimmy watches on triumphantly.

                             TROY
                        (desperate)
                   Alicia?

Jimmy's face drops, he reels back.

With a YELL, Cassie rushes Jimmy and drives the screwdriver
right between his shoulders.

Troy lowers Alicia to the ground.

                             TROY (CONT'D)
                        (crying)
                   I'm sorry.

Jimmy drops to the ground, arms flailing, unable to reach the
screwdriver. He crawls towards Alicia. WEEPING, he cradles
her. He loved her in his own way.

Troy picks up the gun, points it at Jimmy.

Jimmy looks up at Troy through tear stained eyes.

                             JIMMY THE FIX
                   Do it!! End it!

Troy's hand wavers, but he's unable to pull the trigger.
Instead, he reaches down, and rips Spider's dented Four Leaf
Glover medallion off Jimmy's chest.

EXT. BOAT HOUSE - NIGHT

Chas and Casanova engage in a bloody close-quarters back and
forth. Blood streams from Chas' nose, but he keeps up a hail
of blows. Casanova gets through with another punch, and blood
gushes from a new wound above Chas' eye.

But Chas pays the pain no heed. He counters with a strong
left to Casanova's jaw, and Casanova falls to one knee.

Chas delivers a powerful uppercut, and Casanova goes down.

NEARBY:

Manfri and Roman also exchange blows, their faces bloodied and swollen. Manfri holds his own, but Roman's military training and huge size give him an advantage. He lands a vicious round-house, and now it is Manfri who drops to his knee.

Roman goes in for the kill, but is hit in the face by the FIST of Chas McGregor.

Roman and Chas are more evenly matched. Chas, a machine, keeps punching. Roman finds himself falling back, wobbling.

Manfri gets back to his feet, nods his thanks to Chas and hits Roman with all his strength. Roman goes down like a puppet with its string cut.

The last of Jimmy's henchmen are carried off into the darkness.

The victorious Gypsies CHEER.

INT. MATERNITY WARD - DAY

Cassie is laid in bed, while Tanya and a bruised Troy CLUCK over BABY BEN.

The door opens, and Chas McGregor enters, carrying a poorly wrapped gift, which he hands to Cassie with a kiss.

Cassie opens the present, to reveals Chas' pendant: "THE KING OF THE GYPSIES."

Tanya and Troy excuse themselves.

INT. HOSPITAL ROOM - DAY

A weak DCI Fordham lies in bed, arms bandaged. The door opens, and he smiles weakly as Tanya and Troy enter the room. Troy tucks a red binder under his arm.

>   DCI FORDHAM
>   I owe you my life.
>
>   TANYA
>   Just clear Troy's name and put
>   Jimmy away for good. Then we'll be
>   even.

Fordham nods. They turn to leave.

>   FORDHAM
>   I'm sorry. For everything I did.

                    TANYA
          Do the right thing now.

INT. PRISON - DAY

Jimmy the Fix is escorted towards a cell to a cacophony of catcalls.

The cell door is opened. A noose awaits.

He looks back to see the two Gypsy Tasker brothers, arms folded, smiling at him.

                    TASKER BROTHER 1
          Chas McGregor sends his regards.

The Tasker brothers pull out shivs, advance on Jimmy, who raises his fists, not giving an inch.

The first Tasker brother attacks, drawing blood, but Jimmy counters with a wicked punch to his stomach.

Jimmy dodges another swipe, but he can't take them both. They knock him down, draw more blood, then roughly grab him and string him up in the noose. His feet scrabble as he's lifted.

Then, at the last moment, another inmate - hulking, tattooed Locomotive Jones, who lost to Spider in his first boxing match - joins the fray and smashes both Tasker brothers with a wicked left-right combo. They retreat, and Locomotive Jones smiles at Jimmy, as he rips down the noose.

                    JIMMY
              (coughing)
          I know you.

                    DYNAMITE JONES
          Yes - Locomotive Jones. You once
          gave me a chance to fight for
          money, before the gavvers sent me
          away.

Jimmy regains his breath, smiles crookedly, and reaches out to shake Locomotive's powerful hand.

                    JIMMY
          Stick with me, and you'll soon have
          another chance.

EXT. BEACH - DAY

The sun shines brightly. Troy pulls the beach scene postcard from his pocket. It is the same beach. He walks towards a modest apartment building nearby.

INT. APARTMENT HALLWAY - DAY

Troy RINGS the doorbell. After a moment, the door is opened by Erin, in hospital scrubs. Her name-plate says "ERIN GLOVER, RN." She's floored to see her father standing there. After a moment, she jumps into his arms. They embrace. Troy cries.

Then, Troy's mobile phone RINGS and he answers.

                    JIMMY THE FIX (V.O)
    This isn't over.

                                        FADE TO BLACK.

Printed in Great Britain
by Amazon